# WIND STORM

'Kalki' is the pen name of Ramaswamy Krishnamurthy (1899–1954), whose career in writing and journalism began as activism during the struggle for Indian independence. He served as editor of the popular Tamil magazine *Ananda Vikatan* before launching *Kalki*. The magazine—and eventually its founder—was named for the mythological tenth avatar of Vishnu to symbolise a vision to 'destroy regressive regimes, express radical thoughts, take readers into new directions, and create a new era'. Kalki wrote several novels, including *Parthiban Kanavu* and *Sivakamiyin Sabadam*, as well as political essays, film reviews, dance and music critiques and scholarly work.

Nandini Krishnan is the author of *Hitched: The Modern Woman and Arranged Marriage* and *Invisible Men: Inside India's Transmasculine Networks*. She has translated two of Perumal Murugan's works into English: *Estuary* and *Four Strokes of Luck*. She was shortlisted for the PEN Presents translation prize 2022 and the Ali Jawad Zaidi Memorial Prize for translation from Urdu 2022. She is an alumna of the Writer's Bloc playwrights' workshop by the Royal Court Theatre, London. Her novel-in-manuscript was a winner of the Caravan Writers of India Festival contest and showcased at the Writers of the World Festival, Paris, 2014.

PONNIYIN SELVAN BOOK 4

# WIND STORM

## KALKI

### TRANSLATED BY NANDINI KRISHNAN

eka

# eka

First published in Tamil as *Ponniyin Selvan*

Published in English in 2025 by Eka, an imprint of Westland Books, a division of Nasadiya Technologies Private Limited

No. 269/2B, First Floor, 'Irai Arul', Vimalraj Street, Nethaji Nagar, Alapakkam Main Road, Maduravoyal, Chennai 600095

Westland, the Westland logo, Eka and the Eka logo are the trademarks of Nasadiya Technologies Private Limited, or its affiliates.

Translation copyright © Nandini Krishnan, 2025

ISBN: 9789360455569

10 9 8 7 6 5 4 3 2 1



Type set by Jojy Philip

Printed at Thomson Press (India) Ltd

# CONTENTS

# 1

# THE 'ELELA SINGHAN' KOOTHU

In the middle of the forest, where trees had grown along the curved fringes of a lake-bed whose water had dried up in years gone by, about a thousand Chozha soldiers had set up camp. They were preparing food in enormous iron vats. The smell of kootanjoru[1], boiling over the raging fires in the kilns the soldiers had improvised to make stoves, wafted through the trees. The men were famished and, in a bid to distract themselves from the delicious aroma until the food was ready to eat, they had been singing and dancing. When their beloved Arulmozhi Varmar made a surprise appearance, their delight knew no bounds. It was with great effort that their commander managed to bring his unruly men under control and seat them in a half circle.

They had cut down a large tree for firewood, and Arulmozhi now used the stump as a throne. He was no longer dressed as a mahout. He had changed into silk robes, and wore chains of pearls around his neck, gold jewellery on his hands and arms, and a crown over his head. Vandiyadevan and Azhvarkadiyaan, along with the commander of this battalion, took their seats around the prince.

The soldiers had decided to present the *Elela Singhan* koothu for the entertainment of the prince. This was a historical tale that had passed into folklore. A thousand years before the events of our story, it was said that a Chozha army had swept through Lanka capturing much of the territory, under the leadership of Elela Singhan. The king of Lanka had been chased deep into the mountains, and was in hiding.

The Lankan king's son, Dushtakamanu, grew up with the dream of recapturing his kingdom from Elela Singhan. Once, when he was a child, his mother saw him sleeping with his limbs contorted and his body folded into itself. She woke him and said, 'My child, why are you sleeping in such an odd position? Why not stretch out your arms and legs?', to which the prince replied, 'Amma, the Tamil soldiers are crowding in on me from one side and the ocean is crowding me from the other. What choice do I have but to fold myself up so I can occupy the least possible space?'

Warrior blood ran in the veins of this child, and when he was old enough to go to war, he gathered an army to attack the Chozha invaders. His band of soldiers was soon decimated by the powerful Chozha army. His remaining men fled.

Dushtakamanu then made a decision. He went up to Elela Singhan's court and said, 'Arase! My small band of soldiers could not stand up to your formidable army. I am the only one who is left to fight. You come from a dynasty of fearless warriors. I now challenge you to a duel. The one who wins, gets the Lankan kingdom. The one who loses, will attain Veeraswargam, a heaven for heroes.'

Elela Singhan was stunned by the young prince's courage. He was moved to agree to the duel, and told his soldiers not to intervene. When news of the duel reached Dushtakamanu's men, those who had fled the battlefield returned to watch their prince. The duel went on and on. Dushtakamanu was driven by the desire to win back his birthright. Elela Singhan, who felt sorry for the young man, found that his heart was not in the battle. He couldn't throw his all into the duel, and was eventually killed.

Once Dushtakamanu was crowned king, he erected a pallipadai[2] in the very place where Elela Singhan had sacrificed his life, and praised the older man's heroism and generosity.

A millennium later, the Chozha soldiers presented this incident as a play before their prince, complete with song and dance. The man who played Elela Singhan was so convincing one wondered whether he had actually dropped dead. The prince and the other members of the audience showed their appreciation for the performance with cries of 'Aahaa!' every now and again.

As the play was being staged, Arulmozhi glanced at Azhvarkadiyaan and asked, 'Tirumalai! The duel between Dushtakamanu and Elela Singhan has been documented through paintings on the walls of the Thamballai temple cave. Did you happen to notice those beautiful pictures?'

'No, aiya. I saw you almost as soon as we entered the streets of Thamballai. There was no time to visit the cave temple,' Azhvarkadiyaan said.

'Aha! You must not miss it. The sculptures and paintings are unlike anything I have ever seen before. Our Senthamizhnadu[3] does have its own art, stone carvings and pictures and everything else, but this little island is a true wonder. They have outshone us in every way,' the prince said.

'Ilavarase! The sculptures and paintings in this land won't go anywhere. One can see them anytime. But the same can't be said of you, can it? We must have arrived at an auspicious hour, to have had that particular luck. Parthibendra Pallavan, who preceded us to Thamballai, was leaving the city, having looked for you and decided you were not here. We saw him on our way,' Azhvarkadiyaan said.

'Yes, the general informed me that my brother's dear friend had come looking for me. Can you guess what his mission was?'

'Of course. Aditya Karikalar has ordered him to bring you back to Kanchi.'

'Adade! Is there nothing you don't know? Let's see. This olai that your friend so carefully brought me ... perhaps you know its contents too?'

'Your sister has written that you must leave for Pazhaiyarai right away. Ilavarase! When Kundavai Devi wrote her missive and entrusted it to this scion of the Vaanar clan, all in great secrecy, I was spying on them from behind the trees.'

Vandiyadevan reached for Tirumalai's back and pinched a roll of fat cruelly.

Azhvarkadiyaan slapped his back and said, 'What an awful forest! There are pests here that bite even after dusk!'

The prince said, sounding somewhat incensed, 'Chhe, chhe! What is this, now? You're spying on my beloved sister herself?'

'It was only because I saw what I did that I took the trouble to escort this chap here carefully. Ilavarase! Only the Buddha knows how difficult my task of ensuring this madman didn't get himself into fights and scrapes on the way was. If we had come through Anuradhapuram, he would never have reached here. He'd have picked a quarrel with someone or the other and got himself killed. Why, he even challenged an elephant in musth to a duel! I had to rescue him from the elephant with my staff for a weapon, and bring him to you in one piece.'

'Oho! So, it was only to bring him to me in one piece that you took the trouble to come to Lanka, is it?'

'No, aiya. For my part, I carry a message for you too.'

'What message is this, now? Don't keep me waiting!' the prince said.

'The prime minister feels it would be prudent for you to remain in Lanka for a while longer,' Azhvarkadiyaan said.

'So, three of my elders have three different instructions for me. Whom should I obey?'

Vandiyadevan interjected at this point. 'Ilavarase! Do forgive me for speaking out of turn, but it is your sister whom you must obey,' he said.

'What makes you say that?' the prince asked.

'Because your heart tells you to do so. Even if you won't follow her instructions, I am bound to. Ilaiya Piraatti has commanded that I bring you back to her one way or another,' said Vandiyadevan.

The prince looked Vandiyadevan up and down, and said, 'I have been praying for so long to find just such an intrepid and outspoken friend as you.'

2

# KILLI VALAVAN'S ELEPHANT

The food was ready right on time, just as the koothu came to an end. Lotus leaves, which had been gathered in huge heaps, were laid out before the warriors. As they were ladled on to the leaves, the fragrance of the hot pongal and vegetable gravy teased the nostrils of the men yet to be served.

Once the soldiers had started eating, the prince made his rounds of the camp, stopping to speak to several of them and ask after their well-being. The chosen ones couldn't contain their joy. Everyone else remarked on how lucky they were for the prince to have spoken to them.

The men of the Chozha army had always nursed great fondness and respect for the young prince. This had grown exponentially of late. They knew the prince had not had an easy time convincing the powers-that-be to send grains and money to sustain the army from Chozha Naadu, when the norm was to loot and plunder conquered territories. And here he was, mingling with the soldiers as if he were one of them. His genuine concern for them was inspiring. His unassuming nature endeared him to them.

Many of the soldiers made excuses to stop the prince and worked up the courage to speak to him on some pretext or the other. They typically asked questions about the plan of action. Most of them resorted to, 'When will we march on Pulathisipura[1]?' The prince responded to some with, 'What is the point of marching on Pulathisipura? Mahindan has run off to Rohana after all, hasn't he?' To others, he said, 'Be patient just a little while longer, let the monsoon end.'

Some soldiers complained that they were simply sitting around, without waging war as was their duty. They were unhappy that they couldn't serve the empire as they should, they said. Others told the prince, 'If you would deign to visit us once a month and speak to us as you're doing now, we promise to be patient.'

Once he had finished his rounds, the prince retired to the tent that had been set up for him, some distance from the rest. He asked Vandiyadevan and Azhvarkadiyaan to accompany him.

'Do you see how determined and motivated these men are? If only we'd had better cooperation from Thanjavur, the entire island of Lanka would have been ours by now. We've lost a golden opportunity. There is no way one can wage war through the monsoon here.

Our soldiers will have to sit around doing nothing for three more months,' he said.

'Ilavarase!' said Tirumalai, 'I'm surprised you're preoccupied by such matters, when the entire Chozha empire is under threat. The kingdom established by Vijayalaya Chozhar, whose realms have expanded under Parantaka Chakravarti and Sundara Chozhar, is about to splinter because of infighting!'

'Yes, yes, here you both are, with important news and here I am, venting away about these unimportant matters. Well, now is the time for you to tell me everything you have to say in detail. Let him go first,' the prince said, pointing at Vandiyadevan.

Vandiyadevan launched into his story right away. He told them everything he had seen and heard since he had first set out from Kanchi. He spoke of the various dangers he had encountered, and put on a great show of not wanting to blow his own trumpet even as he went on to do exactly that, telling them of the tricks and stunts he had pulled off.

He finished with, 'Aiya, they have all but imprisoned your father. His close friends, trusted lieutenants and suzerain kings are plotting a terrible conspiracy. The empire is in such danger as you cannot even fathom. You must leave right away and come with me to Pazhaiyarai. Every moment is precious.'

Then, Azhvarkadiyaan began his own tale. He confirmed everything that Vandiyadevan had said, and added several details. He also told them about the secret meeting that had taken place by the pallipadai at Tiruppurambiyam and on which he had spied. He then reiterated that the prime minister had said it was best for the prince to stay away from the Chozha Naadu, which was already simmering.

'The prime minister desires not simply that you avoid returning home but that you don't set out on further conquest in this land. He has asked that you gather your armies and settle them in northern Lanka. Soon, the conspirators will come out and show their true colours. We will need all the men and armies that we can muster to counter them. It is the prime minister's opinion that the soldiers in Lanka will come in handy at that time. The Kaikkola army, the Vellaalar army and the Vanniyar army stationed in Pandiya Naadu have declared that they are happy to lay down their lives in your service. The prime minister has ordered me to convey this to you,' Azhvarkadiyaan said.

'Tirumalai! What does your guru have planned? Has he remade himself in the mould of Chanakya of Pataliputra? Is he Chanakya of Anbil now? He wants me to go to war against my family and friends, does he?' Arulmozhi Varmar asked angrily.

'No! Aiya! Aniruddha Brahmarayar has said no such thing. All he wants is for the men who are conspiring against the emperor, the men who are planning treason, to be punished when the time is right. Isn't it your duty to join such an effort?' Tirumalai said.

'Surely, that is not my decision to make? If there is indeed a conspiracy afoot, is it not up to the emperor to counter it? How can I join the war effort without explicit instructions from my father?' the prince asked.

Vandiyadevan piped up at this point. 'Ilavarase! Your father is not at liberty to do as he wishes. The Pazhuvettaraiyar brothers have, as I told you, all but imprisoned him. No one can approach him without their permission. No one can get a message through to him. Nothing gets past them. Your brother, for his part, has sworn that he will never set foot in Thanjavur. Does it not, then, fall to you to protect the empire? Isn't it your duty to come with me to Pazhaiyarai at once?' he asked.

'What is the point of the prince going to Pazhaiyarai? That makes no sense to me at all,' Azhvarkadiyaan said.

The prince thought for some time and said, 'The desire for land is an ugly monster. The lust for power, the craving to rule territory, has wrought many sins in this world. I have just returned from Simhagiri, as you know. Do you know the history of the fort there?'

'I've never heard this story,' Vandiyadevan said.

'Listen, then. About five hundred years ago, a king called Dhatusena ruled Lanka. He had two sons, Kasyapa and Moggallana. Kasyapa conspired with the king's most trusted general and usurped the throne. He threw his own father in prison. Moggallana escaped to Tamizhagam by sea. Soon after, the conspirators killed Dhatusena in the cruellest possible way, by immurement. Now, Kasyapa was haunted by the fear that his half-brother and the rightful heir to the throne, Moggallana, would return and avenge their father. So, he marched to Simhagiri. He figured that it would be impossible for enemies to approach a fort built on such a steep hill. He spent eighteen years of his life in hiding, closeted away in the Simhagiri fort. One fine day, Moggallana gathered an army with help from the Pandiyan emperor and landed in Lanka. He began to march towards Simhagiri. Kasyapa lost his mind when he heard this. Having spent eighteen years hidden inside the fort, he found himself fuelled by the courage that only insanity can bring. He threw open the gates and marched out to his own death. And in this fort, built by such a despicable man, by a man who killed his own father by walling him in, are paintings of indescribable beauty. I had the chance to see them when I escorted the pilgrims from China there. Adadaa! How does one even begin to speak about the wonder of such art? It has been centuries since those artists painted on the walls, and yet, the colour remains unfaded, as if those scenes were finished just yesterday.'

'Aiya! Will you permit me a question?' Azhvarkadiyaan asked.

'Why not? Of course.'

'The Simhagiri fort is still in the enemy's hands, isn't it?'

'Yes. I have no plans to capture it for now. Such a venture will only lead to a lot of pointless deaths.'

'That is not why I asked, aiya. What I meant was … is it prudent for you to enter a fort that is under enemy control? Why did you have to disguise yourself as a mahout and accompany the Chinese pilgrims there? I couldn't believe my eyes when I saw you sitting on the elephant's back. It was only from your eyebrows that I recognised you. Is it right for you to be so careless with your life? How could you court such danger?'

'What makes my life so precious? How many Chozha warriors have already laid down their lives in Lanka?'

'They lost their lives on the battlefield. You took an absolutely unnecessary risk.'

'It was not unnecessary. I had two reasons. One was that I have been wanting to see the legendary paintings of the Simhagiri fort for a very long time. Today, I've fulfilled that desire.'

'And the second, ilavarase?'

'The moment Parthiba Pallavar reached Tirikonamalai, I was given news of his arrival. I didn't wish to meet him. Because …'

'Because …?'

'I was also aware that the prime minister had come to Mathottam. I expected a message from him. When one receives instructions from two of one's elders, one is bound to obey the instruction one hears first, isn't it?'

Vandiyadevan said in delight, 'A-ha! Well said! So, my team wins!'

'Arase! This man has fooled you with his cunning.'

'He hasn't fooled me. I chose to be fooled. I saw him shove the soldier, who was sent to escort you to me, off his horse and mount the steed himself. I wanted to teach him a lesson ...'

'Some lesson you taught me! Several lessons, each with such force. My chest and back hurt at the memory! Is this how one treats a messenger? Well, that's quite all right, as long as you will come to Pazhaiyarai with me ...'

'An old song comes to mind. Tirumalai! Perunkilli Valavan was among my ancestors. He had an elephant that was a wonder in itself. One of its legs was stationed in Kanchi, another in Thanjai, yet another in Eezha Naadu and the fourth in Uraiyur.

'A poet once sang of this elephant:

*Kachchi oru kaal midhiyaa*
*Oru kaalaal thaththuneer thanthanjai thaanmidhiya*
*pitraiyum*
*Eezham oru kaal midhiya varume nam*
*Kozhiyar Ko Killi kaliru.*


*A leg in Kanchi and at the very same time*
*Another leg in Thanjai with its bubbling river—and yet*
*Another raised to claim Eezham, approaches*
*The great elephant of our Kozhiyar[2] king.*

'There are herds upon herds, each with thousands of elephants, in Lanka. But what is the point? If only one, just one, were like the elephant of the poet's imagination, I could be at Kanchi and Pazhaiyarai and Madurai and Lanka, all at the same time, no?'

Vandiyadevan and Azhvarkadiyaan couldn't stop laughing at the idea of such an elephant.

When they had finally wiped the tears from their eyes, Tirumalai said, 'But, as you yourself pointed out, no such elephant exists. What are you going to do?'

'Why do you ask? Haven't we already decided he's coming with me to Pazhaiyarai?' Vandiyadevan said.

'Stop fighting now. We'll go to Anuradhapuram tomorrow. I'll have to meet Parthibendra Pallavar there. I can only make a decision once I've heard him out,' the prince said.

# 3

## THE STATUE'S MESSAGE

Even before sunrise the next day, Arulmozhi Varmar, Azhvarkadiyaan and Vandiyadevan were on their way to Anuradhapuram. They walked along the forest path for a while and then reached the main road, the Rajpath. It surprised Vandiyadevan that the prince had chosen not to bring along an escort of his soldiers for protection.

Vandiyadevan had never in his life experienced anything like this journey. To walk on the broad avenue, bordered by trees on either side, in the cool morning air, was a joy in itself. He was thrilled with himself at having successfully completed the task which the princess had assigned to him in Pazhaiyarai.

Was that all? He had yearned for years to meet the golden boy, beloved of everyone in Chozha Naadu, and that wish had now been realised. He had actually met the prince to whose courage and courteousness people sang paeans.

And what a meeting it had been! He could now vouch that Arulmozhi Varmar was indeed cut from a different cloth. The way the prince had stunned him by suddenly turning the horse around and attacking him! This must be the secret of his successes on the battlefield. His modus operandi was to catch the enemy unawares, at a time and place where they were least expecting an assault. But that could not be the only reason for his numerous victories. He charmed everyone with his affability and humility. The way he spoke to the soldiers, the respect he accorded the commanders ... the prince was truly unique.

And it wasn't only the soldiers he charmed. The people of the very land he had conquered were taken with him. They were free to walk the streets as before, and there was barely any sign of the country having witnessed a violent war. Villagers went about their business as if it were peacetime, with no sign of anxiety or sorrow on their faces. Why, the laughter of women and children could be heard every so often. How bizarre this was!

Vandiyadevan thought back to the anger the prince's insistence that the conquered land not be plundered and that food and provisions be sent from Chozha Naadu for the army had evoked in the Pazhuvettaraiyar brothers, and how they had complained to the emperor. He couldn't help comparing Aditya Karikalar's barbaric warmongering with Arulmozhi Varmar's considerate conquest. He could never have imagined that he would ever find fault with his leader and commander Aditya Karikalar. However, the contentment on the faces of the people who lived along the Rajpath and the happy sounds of everyday life prompted him to question the methods the crown prince employed. Ammamma! Could one imagine such a scene in the kingdoms on which Aditya Karikalar marched? All one heard were screams of terror and wails of grief.

Vandiyadevan's heart ached to speak to the younger prince at length, so that he could ask his opinion on various subjects to do with conquest and governance. But where was the time and space for conversation when they were rushing along on horseback? Well, an opportunity did arise.

When they had almost reached Anuradhapuram, Vandiyadevan noticed a gigantic statue of the Buddha by the roadside. He had seen many such statues, and would not normally have thought anything of it. But Ponniyin Selvar reined in his horse as they approached the statue, and so Vandiyadevan was forced to follow suit. Azhvarkadiyaan, who was leading the way, saw that the two of them had stopped by the statue and turned his horse around to join them.

Ponniyin Selvar studied the imposing statue keenly for some time.

'Adada! What an incredible statue this is!' he said.

'I find nothing incredible about this,' Vandiyadevan said. 'You can't find a single street in this entire kingdom that doesn't have the shadow of a Buddha statue falling over it. Whatever purpose do these serve?'

The prince smiled at Vandiyadevan. 'You speak your mind. There is no filter and no hesitation. I like that,' he said.

'Ilavarase! Vandiyadevar has only just adopted the habit of speaking the truth,' Tirumalai said. 'Today is the first day of this new lifestyle.'

'Vaishnavare! This is known as "sagavaasa dosham"—one is influenced by the company one keeps. Ever since I met you in Veeranarayanapuram, there has been a constant kalpana thandavam on my tongue—everything I spoke was fuelled by imagination, exaggeration and distortion. Since I met the prince, though, my tongue has turned honest,' Vandiyadevan said.

Their war of words was lost on the prince, who was staring at the statue as if mesmerised.

'There are only two figures in the world that lend themselves fully to the skill of the sculptor. One is Nataraja. And the other is the Buddha,' he said.

'But why is it that we don't have Nataraja statues of such mammoth proportions back in Chozha Naadu?'

'The ancient kings of Lanka were truly great men. The swathe of territory over which they ruled might have been small, but their hearts were large and their faith was all-encompassing. They built these enormous statues and stupas and viharas as a mark of their belief in and surrender to the Buddha. When I see such imposing manifestations of religious fervour here and compare them to the little Shiva temples in Chozha Naadu, I feel embarrassed,' Ponniyin Selvar said.

With that statement, he slid off his horse and approached the statue. He looked at the feet of the statue and at the lotus buds that had been offered in prayer. He then bowed low, touched the feet of the statue, prayed and returned to his horse.

The horses now ambled along towards Anuradhapuram.

'What's going on? It appears the prince is all set to convert to Buddhism?' Vandiyadevan whispered to Tirumalai.

The prince heard him and looked at the two of them. He then said, 'There's a reason for my faith in the Buddha. The feet of the statue had an important message for me!'

'Aha! Neither of us heard this message!'

'It was conveyed to me in silence.'

'What is the message? May we know?'

'The flowers at the lord's feet told me that tonight, at the twelfth naazhigai, I must be near the Simhadhara lake,' Ponniyin Selvar said.

# 4

## ANURADHAPURAM

As the sun was setting, they neared Anuradhapuram. Even from some distance Vandiyadevan found himself astounded by the wonders of this ancient Lankan capital. He had heard many, many people describe the city before. These descriptions had teased his imagination into envisioning the city. But the reality defied both imagination and description. He was lost for words. Ammamma! How forbidding the city wall was! It stretched for so long that one could barely make out where it began to curve around. And even above that high, high wall, there were gopurams and stupas and domes and minarets of mansions that towered into the sky with regal splendour. How could a single city, a single wall contain within itself so many buildings of such beauty? Why, Kanchi, Pazhaiyarai and Thanjai could never compete with this grand city! Perhaps the Pataliputra of Ashoka's time, the Ujjaini of Vikramaditya's time and the Kaverippattinam of Karikaal

Valavan's time were comparable to Anuradhapuram? It certainly was unrivalled in the present era.

As the entrance gates of the city appeared before them, the crowd on the approach road began to grow. There were Tamilians and Sinhalese, monks and householders, men and women, and boys and girls. There was a sense of celebration in the air, as if they were going to a temple festival. Some of the people in the crowd seemed to notice our three travellers. They even pointed at them a couple of times. Once Ponniyin Selvan saw this, he subtly signalled to his two companions that they should move off the Rajpath. They took a shortcut through the trees, until they came to a little nook.

The prince brought his horse to a halt and turned to the others. 'These poor animals have had a long journey. Let them rest for a bit. We'll enter the city once dusk falls,' he said.

The three men dismounted and sat on a fallen boulder.

'There's such a huge throng of people headed to the city,' Vandiyadevan mused. 'Is there some sort of festival coming up?'

'Today is the biggest, grandest tiruvizha[1] of all in this kingdom,' the prince said.

'I heard a war was being fought in Lanka. But all I see here are celebrations!' Vandiyadevan said.

'Didn't you say Sri Jayanti[2] was being celebrated in Pazhaiyarai?'

'Yes, but Pazhaiyarai is in Chozha Naadu.'

'And Anuradhapuram is in Eezha Naadu. What of it? Sundara Chozhar rules in Chozha Naadu now. And his sengol[3] rules in Eezha Naadu now.'

'But apparently the enemy has not yet been vanquished ...?'

'The enemy is in hiding. How are the commonfolk responsible for the actions of their rulers? Let us reserve the battlefield for battles and cities for celebrations! Tirumalai ... what is your opinion?' the prince asked.

'Well, there are outsider enemies here, and insider enemies there. An insider threat is the more dangerous of the two. It is the humble opinion of this devotee of the lord that the prince remain here and deal with the battles and celebrations in which the outsiders indulge!' Azhvarkadiyaan said.

'What an idea! If an insider threat is more dangerous, shouldn't the prince be there to deal with it? The bravest of warriors belong in the most dangerous of arenas, don't they?' Vandiyadevan said.

'Does bravery imply that one should get oneself caught in the nets woven by conspirators and murderers? If that is so, why didn't you—bravest of brave warriors—go get yourself caught there? Why did you escape and land up here?' Azhvarkadiyaan demanded.

'Enough, enough! The two of you don't start a battle here!' Arulmozhi Varmar said.

The three men approached the city gates once dusk had fallen. No one was being stopped and questioned at the entrance. The guards stood by and allowed pilgrims and visitors to file in. The three main characters of this section of our story blended in with the masses and found themselves inside Anuradhapuram.

The streets were abuzz with excitement. The prince and his companions barely had room to move among the sea of people. Chants of 'Sadhu, sadhu!' rose into the night sky.

Vandiyadevan noticed that several of the viharas and temples had been reduced over time to ruin. Many were under renovation. The work must have been undertaken at the instance of the prince. Why was Ponniyin Selvar showing such consideration to a defeated people, Vandiyadevan wondered. Sinhalese kings had been waging war against Tamizhagam for a thousand years. Having captured the enemy's stronghold, any conqueror ought rightly to have destroyed the city and its buildings, burnt the place down and reduced the homes and memories of its residents to rubble. And here the prince was, renovating buildings that had been neglected by the inhabitants of this land and allowing them to observe their religious festivals!

Surely, he must have an ulterior motive for such strange behaviour? What could it be? A sudden thought crossed Vandiyadevan's mind. Yes, that must be it, he said to himself. The prince had no birthright in Chozha Naadu. Aditya Karikalar had been named the crown prince. Madurantaka Devar was gearing up to challenge him. It appeared Arulmozhi had plans to establish his own rule over this island. Who knew, this wish of the prince's just might come true. The astrologer of Kudandai had said, hadn't he, that the prince was like the Dhruva nakshatra, the pole star, and that those who put their faith in him would never know want? Vandiyadevan thought again how lucky he was to have made the acquaintance of such an admirable ruler.

They stopped at an old building whose outer halls had crumbled. The spot was somewhat removed from the main streets, and was relatively deserted. They dismounted. The prince clapped thrice. As if by magic, a door opened on one side of the building, and a path appeared. It was too dark to make anyone out. The prince entered the pitch-black corridor and moved forward. Vandiyadevan glanced behind to see what had become of the horses.

'The horses know the way,' the prince said, reached for Vandiyadevan's hand and dragged him forward.

They walked in the dark for some distance, and then they saw a slight glimmer of light. Soon, a brightly lit room appeared. Vandiyadevan realised that these were the interiors of an old palace.

'We must be on our guard here. This is the antapuram of Mahasena Chakravarti. Who knows, the emperor might make a sudden appearance and chase us all out!' the prince said, with a laugh.

'Who is Mahasenar?' Vandiyadevan asked.

'An emperor who ruled here six hundred years ago. He is famous for the work he did to ensure the welfare of the public. People believe his ghost still roams this town, looking out for them. They worry that his spirit will be cold at night without adequate clothing, and so they leave clothes hanging on the trees for him to wear. No one has lived in this palace after him. It has always been left empty,' the prince said.

There were servants about, to serve the prince and his companions. Once they had bathed and eaten, they moved to one of the upper terraces of the palace. They chose to sit at a spot that offered them a view of the entire city, but was well-hidden from prying eyes. No one could spot them from the road below.

'Aiya, you said the Buddha statue sent you a message, asking you to be somewhere at the twelfth naazhigai?' Vandiyadevan said.

'We have time. The moon has just risen. You see the dagoba there? Once the moon rises to the height of its tip, we'll leave,' the prince said.

He pointed at a huge dagoba stupa, high as a hill.

The stupas that had been built in places sanctified by the corporeal relics of Lord Buddha were known as 'dhatu garbhas', a term which had been corrupted over time to 'dagoba'.

'Why did they build such enormous structures, though?' Vandiyadevan asked.

'Well, first they built large stupas to show the world just how great the Buddha was. Later, the kings wanted to show the world just how great they themselves were, so they built even larger stupas,' the prince said.

Not long after, there was a roar that could have rivalled the sound of the ocean. Vandiyadevan turned, startled. In the distance, he could make out a sea of people, rolling in endless waves through the streets. And like black whales in that sea were hundreds of elephants, walking among them. Lamps carried by the people shone like the reflection of stars on the sea. There must be hundreds of thousands of people, Vandiyadevan thought.

'What is this! Has the enemy gathered an army to attack us?' he cried.

'No, no, this is the greatest of this kingdom's celebrations—the Perahara Tiruvizha,' the prince said.

As the procession neared their palace, Vandiyadevan's astonishment grew. He had never encountered such a sight in his life.

The assembly was led by a group of about thirty elephants, decorated with ceremonial headpieces made of gold. In the centre was an elephant taller and larger than all the rest, bearing a howdah studded with navaratna gems and a casket with a golden umbrella on top. On the elephants surrounding this leader sat Buddhist monks, waving chamaras with silver handles. The devotees walking among the elephants carried flares, torches and lamps of various sizes and types, and the golden jewellery of the elephants and the silver handles of the chamaras glinted in their light.

Behind the elephants was a large assembly of people. Of them, about a hundred were in ceremonial clothes, wearing the stage make-up of actors. They carried all sorts of drums and cymbals, and among them were dancers who seemed possessed. Appappa! What a dance it was! The Devaraalan and Devaraatti, who had performed in the Kadambur palace, were as nothing compared with this lot. Every now and again, some of the dancers would soar high into the air and turn two, even three, somersaults airborne before landing on their feet again. When they did this, the bejewelled waistbelts they wore swirled around their clothes, making them appear like the decorative umbrellas that were used in temple festivals. Imagine the sight of a hundred dancers spinning in the air all at once! Two eyes are not enough to take it in, are they? One would need at least two thousand eyes to observe it all. As for the music, two thousand ears won't do, one would need two hundred thousand to absorb the deafening sound of the various percussion and wind instruments.

Behind this group came another thirty elephants, decorated just as the previous lot had been, with their leader carrying an ornate golden box in his howdah, which was being fanned by the chamaras of the monks who sat in the howdahs of his entourage.

The elephants were followed by yet another group of dancers.

However, there was a difference. Among them walked actors dressed as Rathi, Manmadha and Shiva with a third eye painted on his forehead.

'What is this, now? Since when has Shiva Peruman started visiting Lanka?' Vandiyadevan asked.

'A Lankan king called Gajabahu escorted Shiva Peruman to Lanka. And since then, the guest has refused to leave,' the prince said.

'O, Veeravaishnavare! You see? Now you see who the greater of the gods is?' Vandiyadevan was asking, when yet another group of elephants came into view.

The dancers behind them counted in their midst actors wearing costumes that brought the image of Garuda to mind—feathers and exaggerated beaks. They swirled and twirled and danced and jumped, even flew.

'Appane, you see now? Our Tirumaal has arrived on his Garuda Vahana!' Azhvarkadiyaan said.

The next group of elephants was followed by dancers bearing swords, spears and other weapons, with which they made a great deal of noise. The 'danaar-danaar' of the swords and spears kept time with the beat of the musical instruments.

The final lot of elephants was followed by dancers who carried enormous cymbals in both hands. When they danced in step, the cymbals let out a synchronised 'kaleer-kaleer'. The dancing reached a frenzy at times, and then slowed down to a graceful, feminine pace.

Vandiyadevan's head was reeling from the sounds and his eyes popping at the sights.

The prince began to tell him the story of this particular tradition.

For all the storied enmity, there had been times in history when the rulers of Tamizhagam and Lanka were on friendly terms too. Among these was the period when Gajabahu ruled Lanka and Senguttuvan ruled Chera Naadu. Gajabahu was invited to Chera Naadu for a festival honouring Kannagi, the wife of Kovalan in the *Silappadikaaram*[4], who is worshipped as a goddess, the patni devadai, a role model for good wives. Gajabahu stayed on to watch other tiruvizhas in Tamizhagam and left impressed. He then invited Senguttuvan to Lanka, and organised a festival for the Chera king, in which he honoured all the Tamil gods— Shiva Peruman, Tirumaal, Kartikeya and the goddess Kannagi. He observed how thrilled his subjects were by the festival and determined that he would conduct such a celebration every year. The Buddha was given the place of prominence and the other four gods were brought in procession after him. The festival had become an annual tradition, which continued even to the present day, the prince said.

'But I don't see any gods?' Vandiyadevan asked.

'Did you see the golden box being carried by the leader of each group of elephants?' the prince asked.

'Yes, I did. Have the gods been locked up in the boxes so they won't escape to Tamizhagam, then?'

Ponniyin Selvar began to laugh. 'No, no,' he said. 'The first elephant that appeared was carrying one of Lord Buddha's teeth in that box. It is the most precious of all Buddhist relics. This human remnant has been locked into a lovely casket and is carried in procession to honour this position,' he said.

'And what was in the boxes that came after?' Vandiyadevan asked.

'They couldn't find the teeth of Shiva, Vishnu, Muruga and Kannagi. So, they've locked up the jewellery the idols of those gods wear in their respective temples,' the prince said.

Vandiyadevan thought for a while and then said, 'Aha … if Periya Pazhuvettaraiyar had led the army here in your stead …'

At this point, the tail of the procession reached the bend in the road and disappeared from view. The din of the instruments began to fade too.

'There is only one naazhigai left for the appointed hour. Come, let's go,' the prince said and got up from his seat.

The three men went down the stairs and onto the street. They began to walk in the direction opposite to that which the procession had taken. The streets were empty. Everyone had gone to participate in the Perahara Tiruvizha.

In a while, they reached a wide lake, so large that its waters were not still but rolled in waves, on which the moonbeams danced like slivers of silver.

As they walked around the lake, the fragrance of shenbagham flowers hit them. There were flowering bushes and plants of all kinds around them. White flowers had fallen in heaps along the banks of the lake. They came across several man-made hillocks and ponds. One pond featured the statue of a lion, with a fountain spouting from its mouth. The prince settled down to wait by this pond.

An image of the Buddha statue they had seen outside Anuradhapuram flashed before Vandiyadevan. The prince had counted the flower buds at the feet of the statue before announcing that they were to be somewhere at the twelfth naazhigai, our hero now realised. The fact that they were buds and not fully bloomed lotuses must have indicated that the appointed hour was at night and not noon. He seemed to recall a vessel with the face of a lion lying by the lotus buds. Aha! So, this was the fountain that the vessel had indicated.

All this was very well. But who had left the message at the foot of the statue, and to what end? What dangers could this adventure pose for the prince? Why had Ponniyin Selvar forbidden them to bring any weapons along? Were they going to witness some sort of love scene now? Why had the prince brought the two of them along for a romantic rendezvous, though?

The idea of romance stirred Vandiyadevan's heart. His mind crossed the ocean and leapt to Pazhaiyarai. Ilaiya Piraatti and Vanathi Devi appeared before his mind's eye.

Vandiyadevan decided to draw out the prince.

'Aiya!' he said. 'Doesn't this place bring to mind an ancient palace garden?'

'True. There *was* a beautiful palace garden here. Dushtakamanu's[5] palace was once adjoined to this very nandavanam. Look there! You can see some parts of the palace still standing, a thousand years later,' the prince said.

Vandiyadevan looked at the crumbling walls and said, 'Perhaps that was the antapuram of the palace. The young princesses and their companions must have come to these ponds to splash about and play.'

'This garden has witnessed another wonder, a millennium ago. Dushtakamanu's son Saliya was walking through these gardens one day, when he saw a woman dip a vessel into this pond to water the plants around her. He fell in love with her. He learnt that she was of low birth, and that her name was Ashokamala. He insisted that he would marry only her, and his father was so angered by the idea that he disinherited the prince. Saliya declared that he would give up the throne to marry Ashokamala. Do you think any prince in this world would ever make such a sacrifice?'

As Ponniyin Selvar spoke, Vandiyadevan was reminded of Samudra Kumari rowing the boat in the sea off Kodikkarai. Aha! Had that girl been on the prince's mind? Was that why he had narrated this tale? He was wondering how he would bring up the subject, when something quite bizarre occurred.

The fountain had a back wall with an alcove. There was a seat inside the alcove that could accommodate two people. In one corner of this little nook, a light suddenly appeared. First, they saw the hand of the torchbearer and then the face of a Buddhist monk.

Vandiyadevan couldn't contain his shock at this magical sight. He was bursting with anticipation as to what would happen next, so much so that he forgot to breathe for some time.

# 5

# THE LANKAN THRONE

The monk looked about himself in the light of the lamp he held. He seemed to note the presence of the prince and his companions, for the next moment the lamp and its glow disappeared. Soon after, they spotted the monk making his way down the main stairs. He approached the prince, and looked at his face in the moonlight.

'Devapriya! Welcome, welcome! The Vaidulya Bhikshu Sangham awaits you. The Mahathero Guru has graced our gathering too. I'm thrilled that you have arrived at exactly the right hour, and you have my heartfelt gratitude for it,' the monk said.

'Adigale[1]! I sense many faults in myself, but failing to keep to my word is not among them. I have never missed an appointment,' Ponniyin Selvar said.

'I learnt that you had not reached by sunset, and I was rather worried,' the monk said.

'If I'd come early, I might have been forced to fail to keep the appointment. That was why I ensured I arrived right on time.'

'You're right, you're right. We, too, are aware that dark clouds have been gathering to suffocate the radiant sun. But those clouds will disperse as dust in the gale of Lord Buddha's compassion and mercy. Well, that's as may be. Who are your companions? Do you know them well? Can they be trusted? Are they men who will forever keep an oath?' the monk asked.

'Adigale! I trust these two friends as much as I trust my two hands. But if you prefer it, I'm happy to leave them behind and walk alone with you,' the prince said.

'No, no. I'm not willing to take on such a tremendous responsibility. It is indeed a place of great safety to which I've been assigned to escort you. However, we will have to travel a long route. Who knows what dangers lurk behind which pillar? I would certainly like your friends to come along to protect you,' the monk said.

Vandiyadevan's heart sang as he heard the prince's words—he trusted him as he trusted his own hand, Arulmozhi Varmar had declared! He, whom the prince had only just met! He felt elated at the thought that he was already considered a confidant. He was also excited by the adventure. Clearly, something of great significance was to occur that night. What could it be?

They followed the monk as he lit their path. They went up the stairs and then circled the building up to a nook in the back wall, which led into a passage. The monk went to a corner and did something. A path appeared before them, with flares lighting the way. The monk took hold of a torch and went on ahead. Once the three other men had entered the chamber, the entryway was sealed again. They could hear the faint sound of the fountain they had seen earlier, emerging from the lion's mouth, and that was the only evidence they had that they had ever stood outside this enormous temple. They could never have imagined that the grand exterior hid inside it this dingy, narrow path they were walking on now. The passage wound its way through subterranean rock, seemingly without end. Their footsteps echoed with a sinister sound. Every now and again, Vandiyadevan wondered whether the prince had been fooled into walking headlong into a trap.

Eventually, the passage began to widen until they arrived at a chamber, beyond which they could see a mandapam. And what a mandapam it was! The flare the monk held only allowed them a dim view of a portion of the hall. But they could see that the pillars were made of marble. There were beautiful sculptures of the Buddha in every corner, in every imaginable pose—sitting, in repose, meditating, blessing devotees, praying ...

They crossed the marble mandapam and entered yet another narrow passage, which opened out onto yet another mandapam, the pillars of which were made of copper. They glowed red as rubies in the flare. Even the roof bore copper plates, with intricate carvings. Buddha statues gazed upon them from every direction.

Next came a mandapam with pillars made of sandalwood. And then another which had ivory pillars. Even as they hurried along, Vandiyadevan reached out to caress a pillar or two from curiosity about the material of which they were made. He wondered at the prince, who paid them no heed at all and seemed entirely focused on the destination.

Having crossed all these grand mandapams, they finally arrived at one made of simple black stone. But it was the largest of the halls, and housed a rather stunning sight. They had only come across statues thus far, not living human beings. But here, they saw a gathering of monks, their faces glowing with the light of devotion. Sitting in state at the peetham was the Mahathero guru. Across from him was a golden throne, studded with navaratna gems. Before the throne was a crown, a sword and a sengol, all of which shone in the light of the many flares that were ensconced along the walls of the mandapam.

As the prince and his companions entered the mandapam, the monks rose as one and chanted:

*Buddhar vaazhga! Dharmam vaazhga! Sangam vaazhga!*

*Long live the Buddha! Long live dharma! Long live the sangam!*

The prince approached the Mahathero guru, who had risen too, and bowed before him.

The Mahathero gestured for the prince to be seated.

'Mahaguru! I am but a boy. You are senior to me in age, knowledge and dharma. I beg that you be seated first,' the prince said.

Once the Mahathero sat down, the prince took a seat too.

'Prince, beloved of the gods! The Mahabodhi Sangam is overjoyed by your arrival. You have taken much trouble to fulfil the conditions we had laid out. This alone is proof that the grace of our Lord Buddha has illuminated your soul,' the Mahathero said in Pali, which the monk who had escorted them translated into Tamil.

Once he had finished, the monks chorused, 'Sadhu! Sadhu!'

'We are greatly indebted to Bharatvarsha, the land that brought our dharma to this island,' the Mahathero said. 'However, for too long, the Chozhas, Pandiyas, the Malabar kings and Kalinga rulers have attacked us with their armies and wreaked havoc on this island. They have destroyed viharas and monasteries and gurukulams, and earned the wrath and curses of the gods. However, it isn't simply the kings of your land but the rulers of our very own island who have wrought destruction on our holy places. They have caused divisions in our sangams. They have destroyed the viharas of the bhikshus who opposed them, and turned them into fodder for fire. Do you know, once upon a time, half of this city—this city which measures two kaadhams in length and a kaadham in width—comprised viharas? But most of them are in ruin now. No ruler has ever ordered that they be renovated or rebuilt. It is you who have the honour of being the first. Prince Arulmozhi Varmar, you are blessed by the divine. The Buddha Mahasangam would like you to know just how much we appreciate this act of yours.'

The prince bowed low in acknowledgement of the Mahathero's praise.

'And that's not all. The Perahara festival has not taken place in this city for a long time, not since the Pandiyas captured it and forced our kings away to Pulathisipura. It is you who have restarted the tradition this year, and made arrangements for the festival to be held. We are delighted with this act too.'

The prince bowed again and said, 'Mahaguru! Please let me know if I can, in any other way, be of service to the Buddha Mahasangam.'

The Mahathero smiled and said, 'Why, yes, indeed, Ilavarase! The Buddha sangam is confident that you will be of great service to us. But before I come to that, I have something important to say. You must know that Lord Buddha had manifested himself in many avatars before his final one as Gautama Buddha. As

Sibi Chakravarti, he embodied compassion in a cruel world. He sliced his own flesh off his bones in order to save the life of a little dove. You claim the Chozha dynasty is descended from Sibi Chakravarti and to this end, you use the title "Sembiyan". But the members of the Buddha Mahasangam have not been able to bring themselves to believe that this is the case. It must be one of the tall stories concocted by sycophants of the throne, we thought. However, having observed you and your acts of devotion, we are forced to concede that Sibi Chakravarti must indeed be an ancestor of the Chozhas. The compassion embodied by our lord must simply have been latent in all those who have come before you. However, it has manifested manifold in you, my prince. We even have an oracle who says ... wait ... look!'

The Mahathero turned, and at a signal from him, several monks went up to another monk, who was collapsed on a chair. They then carried the chair, with the monk still on it, up to the peetham. The monk's body was trembling. His hands shivered, his legs shuddered, his torso shook. His head lolled back and his teeth ground against each other. His lips quivered. His eyes were red and his eyebrows danced.

'All thirty-three crore devas have possessed the spirit of this monk,' the Mahathero said. 'Do you hear what they have to say?'

The monk who was in a trance opened his mouth and began to speak. A babble of pronouncements in a babel of languages spilled from his tongue.

Once he had stopped speaking, the Mahathero said, 'All thirty-three crore devas bless you. They speak of Emperor Ashoka, who once ruled nearly all of Bharatvarsha and spread Buddhism across the world. The devas say you will rule over an empire quite as large. Just as Ashoka sat on the throne of Pataliputra and ensured good deeds were done in the name of this religion, you too shall carry out great deeds from this ancient city of Anuradhapura! The devas demand that you fulfil this destiny. What is your response?'

'Mahaguru,' the prince said, 'the devas are all-powerful. They will see that their will is done. But I don't understand what role I must play in all this.'

'I will tell you,' the Mahathero said, and gestured for the possessed monk to be carried back to his place. Once the monks had done his bidding, he said, 'Ilavarase, you see the throne and crown and sengol before you. All the kings who have ruled this land have sat on this throne, worn this crown and held this sengol, and sought the blessings of the Buddha Mahasangam. It is this throne that witnessed the coronation of Dushtakamanu, Devanampiya Tissa and Mahasena. It is this crown that graced their heads. It is this sengol that they held aloft. And all these three, which have created and consecrated rulers for a whole millennium, now await you. Are you willing to sit on this throne, wear this crown and hold this sengol?'

Vandiyadevan could not believe his ears. Such was his joy that he wanted to carry the prince to the throne right away. But the prince's expression remained unchanged.

The prince said, in the same calm tone he had been using all along, 'Adiarchaka! How is that even possible? King Mahinda who was crowned on this very throne is still alive, isn't he? Even if one doesn't know where he is ... '

'Ilavarase! It is the will of the gods that the ruling dynasty of Lanka change. It will happen as they wish. From the lands where the Ganga dances up to this kingdom that Vijayaraja founded, so many, many maharajas have been born and have proven themselves worthy of the title. They have followed the path of righteousness. However, this kingdom has been cursed, for its rulers have fallen foul of righteousness. They have wrought terrible deeds. Fathers have killed sons and sons have killed fathers; brothers have killed each other; mothers have killed daughters; daughters-in-law have killed mothers-in-law. The gods have shown that people born of such blood are not fit to spread Buddhism. Mahinda has lost his right to the throne of Lanka. When a dynasty ends, it is our sangam that has the right to choose a new dynasty to take over the rule. The members of this sangam wish to anoint you as our king. If only you would consent to this, we can have the coronation ceremony tonight … '

The hall was silent as the centre of the earth, as the bottom of the ocean. Vandiyadevan could barely contain his excitement.

Ponniyin Selvar stood up from his seat and bowed before the monks assembled in the hall.

Vandiyadevan ached to crown the prince himself, once the latter had accepted the monks' request and assumed his position on the throne.

'O great ones,' the prince said, 'I bow before you. I bow before your generosity in placing your trust in a greenhorn like me and offering me this ancient throne. I bow before the love you have for me. However, what you ask of me is not within my power to decide. I came here in accordance with the wishes of my father, Sundara Chozha Chakravarti. I can do nothing further without knowing his will.'

The Mahathero said, 'Ilavarase! Do you not know that your father has lost all free will and even freedom, and is as a prisoner in his own kingdom?'

'True, my father has been laid low by illness. He has lost the use of his legs. However, I am bound by the will of those who rule in his name and under his authority. If I were to ascend this throne without their consent, I would be a traitor to the kingdom and a traitor to the king.'

'If this is how you see it, we are happy to send a delegation to Thanjavur. Your father thinks highly of Buddhism. He will not oppose our wishes.'

'But what about the people of this kingdom? How does anyone have the right to offer the throne to somebody without their consent?' the prince asked.

'The people of this kingdom would consider it the greatest of honours for you to be their king.'

'Even if it were the case that everyone had consented and that everyone would be happy for me to be king, the person whose wishes I most respect is my sister. My mother birthed me. The river Ponni saved my life. But it was my sister who nourished my mind, who opened my eyes to the world within and without. And there is yet one voice that is more powerful than hers—the voice of my conscience. Mahapurushas! My heart is not able to accept the great honour you have chosen to bestow upon me. Please do have the grace to forgive me.'

Silence reigned in the great hall yet again.

Vandiyadevan could hear his blood pulsing. His nerves felt raw, his heart wouldn't stop thumping.

It was a while before the Mahathero finally spoke. 'Ilavarase,' he said. 'Your response has not quite taken me by surprise. I must have expected this answer. This is the very reason you are the king most fit to rule this land. We, who have studied the scriptures, have little doubt on this account. Your sense of righteousness, which precludes your accepting our offer, is what makes you the right choice for the throne. We do not wish to force your hand. We will give you time to think it over. After a year has passed, we will send you a message, just as we did this time. And we will await your final decision then. But we ask that you keep this in mind—this beautiful city of Anuradhapuram has seen much war. Many, many viharas have been reduced to rubble. But the Mahabodhi Vihara where we are now assembled has never been affected. This is because it has been carved underground. The only ones who know the way here are the heads of the various Buddha sangams who are present at this gathering. No one can reach this spot without one of us for an escort. It is the norm that the kings of Lanka are called once, just once, to be crowned by the members of our sangam. No one has come here twice. This hallowed site is subject to great secrecy. We ask that neither you nor your friends breathe a word about your having come here and left, about the events of this evening. If you flout the law of secrecy, you will be the object of the gods' wrath.'

'Mahaguru, there will be no call for wrath. I gave my word even before we started on this journey that we would be bound by secrecy. I have never gone back on my word,' Ponniyin Selvar said.

Half a naazhigai later, the three men were back on the streets of Anuradhapuram, walking in the moonlight. Vandiyadevan, who had been keeping his peace throughout their time in the vihara, could no longer dam the flow of his questions.

'Chozha Naadu might have gushing rivers and lush landscapes, but could it ever equal Lanka? And you, you who were offered the throne of this land, kicked it away! What madness is this? And what does one say about the wisdom of the monks who offered it to you? I was there, standing as a pillar among those pillars. They might as well have offered *me* the throne!' he fumed.

The prince tried to console him. 'I told you the story of Dushtakamanu's son Saliya who gave up the throne for his love of Ashokamala, didn't I?' he asked. 'Didn't you listen to that story? Didn't you understand the message it contained?'

'Yes, yes, I listened, I understood. Who is your Ashokamala, then? Which woman are you in love with who comes between you and the throne?' Vandiyadevan demanded.

'Not one woman but two. I'm love with two women called Satya and Dharma. It is for them that I refused the throne.'

'Ilavarase, you have the appearance of a young man and the speech of an ancient soul on the brink of death.'

'Who knows who is ancient among us, and who is closest to death?'

As the prince uttered these words, they were passing by an old, dilapidated building. Across from the road, there was a sudden sound, the urgent clapping of hands. They looked in that direction, and saw a figure standing there.

'Come this way,' the prince said, as he crossed the street towards the figure.

His companions followed him. They had walked halfway across the street, when a thunderous noise behind them made them turn. One of the balconies of the dilapidated mansion they had just passed was crumbling and spewing debris on to the very spot where they had been standing a moment before. If they hadn't crossed the road, they would have been crushed under the load. An instant had stood between three lives and death. And what lives too!

*Who knows who is ancient among us, and who is closest to death?*

The prince's words echoing in his ears, Vandiyadevan stood frozen, staring at the rubble.

Arulmozhi and Azhvarkadiyaan had already crossed the road. When he went to join them, he clearly saw the face of the person who had clapped, as the moonlight shone upon the group.

*What madness is this?* he thought. *How is this even possible? How could Nandini, whom I last saw at the Pazhuvettaraiyar palace, be here on a street in Anuradhapuram? And why must she stand here at midnight?*

Before he could look again, the figure had disappeared. Only his two companions stood by the road.

# 6

## 'WHO VALUES ONE'S WORTH?'

Vandiyadevan hurried towards the spot where he had just seen the prince with 'Nandini'. Even before he'd reached that point, doubts began to rise in his head. Was she indeed Nandini? She wasn't dressed in the grand saris and ornate jewellery the Pazhuvoor Rani favoured ... why, she had an ascetic simplicity about her! But her face ... it was all Nandini ... yet, there was something different about her. What was it that distinguished her from Nandini?

Vandiyadevan saw her now, slipping into the shadows of a house by the roadside. He tried to pursue her, but the prince caught his arm and stopped him.

'Aiya? Who is that woman? I'm sure I've seen her before,' Vandiyadevan said.

Azhvarkadiyaan, who had joined them by now, said, 'That woman must be the guardian deity of Chozha Naadu. Look over there ... if we had remained at that spot ... if she had not signalled for us to cross the road, why, we would have reached the lotus feet of Lord Buddha by now!'

They turned to look at the spot where the debris had fallen. A chunk of the balcony had fallen on the road, and now resembled a small hill. Not even an elephant could have escaped being crushed to a horrid death under it. What chance did three mere humans stand?

'Our guardian deity timed the clapping of her hands rather well,' Ponniyin Selvar said.

'Ilavarase! Whom did you say that lady was?' Vandiyadevan asked.

'Whom did you think she was? What made you attempt to follow her?' the prince asked.

'The Vaishnavite said she was the guardian deity of Chozha Naadu. She struck me as a goddess in the avatar of a shield protecting the Chozha dynasty,' Vandiyadevan said.

'What do you mean by that? Whom do you think she was?'

'I don't know if it was simply an illusion. But for a moment, I thought she was the young wife of Periya Pazhuvettaraiyar, Nandini Devi. Did you both not think so?' Vandiyadevan asked.

'I didn't get a good look. But you must have been hallucinating. How could the Pazhuvoor Rani possibly be here?' Azhvarkadiyaan asked.

'He calls it a hallucination. But perhaps it is an optical illusion. It *has* sometimes struck me that the resemblance between those two faces is quite extraordinary,' the prince said. 'Come, let us walk as we speak.'

The three men now chose to walk in the centre of the road, in the moonlight, rather than in the shadows by the side.

After a while, Vandiyadevan asked, 'Ilavarase! What did that lady tell you after she called you to her side?'

'She told me two men I should consider my enemies had come in search of me. And that they were looking for the right opportunity to kill me.'

'Adi paavi! Was she referring to the two of us?' Vandiyadevan fumed.

Ponniyin Selvar laughed and said, 'No, she didn't specify that it was the two of you. But it doesn't worry me if she was indeed referring to you. The devi has told me my lifeline is rather strong. And she has herself saved me from death several times in the past.'

'Aiya! I know who those two enemies are. They were accompanying Parthibendra Pallavar on his search for you. I saw two figures inside the building which has now collapsed. It must have been those two,' Tirumalai said.

'Aiya! Vaishnavare! Why didn't you say so before? Go on, now! I'm going to go search in the rubble!' Vandiyadevan said, and made to run back the way they had come.

The prince stopped him again, and said, 'There is no hurry. We can't possibly find them in the rubble either. Let's not worry about that now. Listen to me— you must remain by my side until I state otherwise, do you hear me? Who knows what dangers lurk around which corner? You, who are courage in human form, are the reason I've decided not to bring along a posse of bodyguards! What am I to do if you abandon me in the middle of the road?'

Vandiyadevan was all but intoxicated by the prince's speech. 'Aiya!' he gasped. 'I will not leave your side for a single moment!'

'And I won't leave *your* side for a single moment,' Azhvarkadiyaan said. 'You're the prince's protector. And I'm your protector.'

It wasn't long before the three men were back at the ruin of Mahasena Chakravarti's palace. The servants had readied their beds in a large hall, equipped with ancient cots that had withstood the vagaries of time. The three men lay down. The windows to one side of the room allowed a beam of moonlight into the room.

'Hundreds of years ago, the emperors of Lanka and their sons and the women of the royal household must have slept in this very hall,' Arulmozhi Varmar said. 'And moonbeams must have peeped in through these very same windows. It must come as a sore disappointment to those moonbeams to see three ordinary men like us occupy the spot that those souls once graced, don't you think, Vandiyadevare?'

'Aiya! You're free to speak of yourself and this Vaishnavite as you please. But I must ask that you never refer to me as an ordinary man again,' Vandiyadevan said.

'Oh, I forgot you are the scion of the ancient Vaanar clan,' the prince said. 'Do forgive my transgression.'

'True, aiya, true! If I were to recite the song a poet composed in honour of one of my ancestors, this Vaishnavite might burn himself to death with jealousy!'

'Oh, you need not worry on that account. Tirumalai is a Tamil patriot. Like Nandi Varman of the Pallava clan[1], he would be only too happy to burn to death for the love of Tamil poetry. Please do honour us with the poem,' the prince said.

It was with some hesitation that Vandiyadevan launched himself into the poem:

*'En kavigai en sivigai*
*En kavasam en thuvasam*
*En kari yeedhu en pari yeedhu*
*Enbare; mankavana*
*Mahavendan vaanan*
*Varisai parisu petra*
*Paavendarai vendar paarththu!*

*'My umbrella! My palanquin!*
*My armour! My flag!*
*My elephant! My horse!*
*They said; as the kings looked upon*

*A procession of poets
Blessed by the generosity of
The great king, the Vaanan.'*

Ponniyin Selvar turned to Tirumalai and said, 'Tirumalai! You're a poet yourself. Would you care to explain the significance of this song to us?'

'Aiya! You wish to put me to the test, I see. Well, here we go. A large number of suzerain kings had gathered outside the palace of the great Vaanar emperor, waiting to meet him. But they were not in much luck. They had to wait until the poets who had preceded them had finished their audience with the emperor. The Vaanar was so pleased with the songs he heard that he rewarded the poets generously. He gave them decorative umbrellas made of the finest material, ivory palanquins, armours of pearl, flags of silver, elephants, horses ... you name it. As the suzerain kings watched the poets leave, they recognised these rewards as the very tributes they had gifted the emperor and cried, raging at the injustice of it all, "Isn't that my umbrella? My palanquin? Oh, that's my elephant! And my horse! And all of those have been given away to these cursed poets!" Ilavarase! Have I interpreted the song right? Have I passed your test?'

'Could you possibly go wrong? Adada! What a wonderful song, what fertile imagination! Who was the great poet who came up with such incredible lines? O scion of the Vaanar clan! Vandiyadevare! However large or small the empire over which your ancestors ruled was, it is of little consequence. All that matters is that they are the subjects of such a beautiful poem. You, who belong to that dynasty, are certainly worthy of this hallowed hall. Let alone Mahasena's cot, you're fit to grace the cot of Dushtakamanu himself!'

'True, aiya, true! I'm worthy of every possible honour one could think of. But who values one's worth these days? Did the monks see fit to bestow the crown of the Lankan kingdom on me? They chose you, only for you to turn it down. Do you know how frustrated I was by it all? I wanted to take the crown and place it on my own head. But what if this Veera Vaishnavite had tried to enter the contest too? That's why I chose not to act on my impulses.'

At this, Arulmozhi Varmar burst into laughter. Although the sound of his laughter warmed Vandiyadevan's heart, our man made a show of being angry and said, 'You think this is a joke? That your laughter makes up for everything? I demand compensation!'

'Aiya! Scion of the Vaanar clan! Didn't I tell you about Satya and Dharma? Do you not think those two are reason enough for me to refuse the throne?'

'I'm already aggrieved by those two, Satya and Dharma. I've decided to break all my ties with them, and have sworn I will never set eyes on them again.'

'Adada! What moved you to make such a drastic decision? Why are you so angry with those two?'

'I'm not angry. Didn't you say you were in love with these two women, Satya and Dharma? So in love with them that you gave up the Lankan throne for them? I don't wish to so much as fantasise about women with whom a friend is in love, that's all.'

This prompted another burst of laughter from the prince. 'I've never come across a man as funny as you are,' he said, wiping his eyes.

'True, aiya. This is all a joke to you. But my heart is on fire. If you didn't want the Lankan throne, couldn't you have pointed at me, standing right by your side, and said, "Give the throne to him"?' Vandiyadevan demanded.

Once Arulmozhi Varmar had recovered from yet another fit of laughter, he said, 'Vandiyadevare! Is it such an easy task to take on a kingdom? And it isn't in good form to accept the title of emperor when it is handed to one by Buddhist monks, is it? This would cause great turmoil. Religious leaders should stick to religion. When they venture into politics, it is neither good for religion nor for governance. Besides, the monks who wanted me to take over the Lankan kingdom do not represent all the sangams here. They belong to a single faction. There are two other factions, each a collective of sangams. If I were to accept the throne from one faction, I would be bound to their will. I would make enemies of the other two factions right away.'

'Does the Vaanar prince now understand the situation?' Azhvarkadiyaan asked.

'Yes, yes, I do. I understand that there are fools in this kingdom too, just as there are fools back home who argue over who the greater god is, Vishnu or Shiva!' Vandiyadevan said.

'All right, don't get into a fight now. It's late. There, you can even hear the people returning from the Perahara celebrations. Let's get some sleep now,' the prince said.

'Sleep will elude me tonight. I can't sleep unless I discover the identity of the woman who saved us from being buried alive.'

'I don't know who she is, myself. But if you'd like, I can tell you what I do know about her. If you wish to listen, come here and sit by me,' the prince said.

7

# KAVERI AMMAN

Vandiyadevan and Azhvarkadiyaan, their curiosity piqued, hurried to sit by the prince's side. The prince began his story:

'Back when I was a child, I'd gone boating on the river Kaveri with my parents. My brother and sister were with us too. Everyone was occupied, talking or playing. I was alone, watching the swirling currents of the river. There were little kadamba flowers that had fallen into the river and were swirling in those currents. As I watched, it struck me that those poor little flowers were in a terrible predicament. They were being sucked into the depths of the river, helpless to defend themselves. I would lean over the side of the boat every now and again to rescue them from the current. Once, I leaned over too far and fell into the river. I went in head first and couldn't breathe anymore. I still remember my head striking the silt at the bottom of the river. I remember panicking and struggling in the water, as the current carried me swiftly to some spot.

'I could hear people screaming in the distance. I gasped for breath. I thought the river was going to carry me to the sea and let me loose, while my parents and siblings went mad with grief. How they would suffer in my absence, I thought. At that moment, I felt two arms scoop me up and hold me close. Suddenly, my head was above water. My hair and eyes and nose and mouth were still streaming with water. And yet, I could see the arms that bore me. And then, I saw the face of the person to whom those arms belonged. It was only for an instant, but that face is indelibly etched on my mind. And it struck me that I had seen that face sometime earlier too. But I couldn't place it.

'I felt those arms hand me over to someone else. And then, I was on the boat again. My mother, father, sister and brother surrounded me. Their sorrow and terror and love and concern overwhelmed me. After a while, everyone began to discuss who it could have been who had saved me from drowning. They asked each other, and they asked me. I looked about myself, but that face with its divine glow was not to be seen. I blinked, unable to answer their questions. In the end, everyone came to the conclusion that it was Kaveri Amman who had saved me. They made arrangements to commemorate the day I'd been rescued with an annual puja in honour of Kaveri Amman.

'But something niggled at me. Whether it had been the Goddess Kaveri herself who had saved me or a mortal woman, my eyes ached for a darshan of that lovely countenance. Every time I walked by the banks of the river or went boating, I would look out eagerly, wondering if she would rise from the waters and grace me with that darshan. As time passed, the conviction that she was a mortal grew stronger. So, every time I attended a tiruvizha, I would scan the faces of the older women in the crowd, hoping to spot her. Later, I realised this was unseemly, and made peace with the fact that I would not see her again. Over the years, I lost the desire to set my eyes upon that face.

'About a year ago, I was appointed the Mahatanda Nayagan of the southern armed forces and arrived at these shores. By this time, Senapati Poothi Vikrama Kesari had already captured several regions of Lanka. Anuradhapuram had changed hands many times over, and was then under the control of Mahinda. Our men had laid siege to the town. When this was going on, I decided to get to know this land and travel to various parts of it. The senapati sent along a guard of a thousand men whom he had handpicked. I went to every part of the land under our control, not leaving out a single forest or field, valley or hill. I got to know the characteristics and character of the land and its people. You must know that there are several little islands off the coast of this one. I visited those too.

'On one of these journeys, we set up camp in a forest a few kaadhams north of this city. We were near Yaanai Iravu.[1] It is at this point that the sea to the east of Lanka and the ocean to the west meet in a narrow canal. Apparently, in the past, herds of elephants would cross over to the northern regions through this pass, which is how it earned its name. While we were staying there, something quite bizarre happened. We would hear a lament in the wee hours somewhere near the camp. We couldn't tell whether the voice was human or animal. But it carried so much sorrow and pain that it would make one's hair stand on end. First, it was the soldiers camped on the outer ring who heard it. They didn't think much of it. Then, it grew louder and penetrated deeper into the camp. Some of our soldiers came and told me about this. I dismissed it, saying scornfully, "Why, are you afraid of ghosts and ghouls? In that case, feel free to go back home and lay your heads in your mothers' laps so you can sleep without fear." They took such umbrage at this that they determined to find out whether the voice belonged to man, animal or spirit. They ran in the direction of the sound. But when they went near, the figure to whom the voice belonged made off at a run. It appeared to be a woman. They were not able to catch her. After that day, we heard the lament regularly.

'I didn't give it much importance at first. But my men would talk about nothing else. Some were overcome by fear. I decided to solve the mystery. I took some men along one night, and went towards the source of the sound. Through the bushes, we saw a woman. She saw us, and stood petrified for a moment. Then, she began to run. An instinct told me we would not be able to catch her if we went as a group. I asked my soldiers to stay behind and set off in pursuit. Once, the woman stopped and glanced back. When she saw I was alone, she turned and stood waiting for me. Now, I felt frightened myself. I hesitated for a moment. Then, I steadied my heart and approached the woman. I could see her face in the moonlight—a face with a divine glow. A tender smile curved its way through her lips. And then it hit me. This was Kaveri Amman! It was she who had saved me from the current all those years ago. I stood as if in a trance for some moments, staring at her face.

'Then, I cried, "Thaaye! Who are you? When did you come here? And why? I have been searching for you for years. Why didn't you come right up to me if you wished to see me? Why are you walking round and round our camp? Why do you break into this lament?" The lady made no reply. I asked this over and over again, but couldn't get a word out of her. Soon, her eyes began to brim with tears. Those tears tore at my heartstrings. I knew she was trying to tell me something. But the words wouldn't come. Strange, unearthly sounds made their way from her throat. And then I realised she was mute. I have never felt as sad as I did at that moment. I didn't know what to do.

The lady came up to me all of a sudden, pulled me into an embrace and then kissed the top of my head. Her tears ran in rivulets through my hair. The next moment, she let me go and started running away. She didn't look back, not even once. I couldn't find it in myself to pursue her either.

'When I returned to the camp, I told the soldiers who had crowded around me to hear the story, "She's no ghost or ghoul, she's an ordinary woman. She seems to have been traumatised by some incident. She is in a world of her own. She's probably lost her mind. If you hear her again, don't go bothering her. Do I make myself clear?"

'All through the next day, I wondered whether we should resume our journey. But I wasn't able to issue the order to fold camp. I couldn't stop hoping that the lady would come see me again. Dusk fell. And then the night deepened. My hopes were not in vain. The lament sounded again, near the camp. I told my men to stay behind and went alone in the direction from which her voice came. She greeted me with the same tender smile. She stared at me for some time, as if drinking in my face. She tried to convey something.

'Then, she took me by the hand and led me forward. I felt no hesitation in following her. As we walked through the forest, she held aside the branches of the trees overhead aside and brushed away the thorns in our path, so I wouldn't be hurt. My heart melted. Soon enough, we arrived at a hut. I could see a lamp flickering inside. In its light, I could see an old man. He seemed ill. His entire body shook, as if from unbearable cold. Every now and again, jerky movements tremored their way through his limbs. His teeth chattered. His eyes grew red and glowed like embers. He was delirious, blathering on without making sense.

'Do you remember how the monk in the underground chamber of the Mahabodhi Vihara shuddered and twitched? They said he was possessed by the gods, who were speaking through him. I was reminded at that moment of the old man in the hut. I wondered whether the monk was indeed possessed by the gods, or by the terrible illness known as the ague. I didn't speak up because that would have destroyed the faith of those monks. I wonder now whether I have erred terribly in permitting the Perahara festival to take place this year. Nearly half the city is in ruins. And if this contagious ague were to spread in this huge gathering of people, what devastation there could be! Whoever is left alive would run away, and this would turn into a ghost town!'

With this, Arulmozhi Varmar sank into silence, as if consumed by some troubling thought.

After a while, Vandiyadevan could no longer contain his impatience and said, 'Aiya! Let's worry about the city later. Tell us what happened in that hut!'

'Nothing happened in the hut. I think the lady didn't want me to linger for long by the old man.

She led me away almost as soon as I had seen him. She then conveyed to me through gestures, which I could intuitively understand. "Don't stay on in these parts. Or, this fever with its chills and shivering will take hold of your camp. Leave immediately." I realised she had gone to so much trouble to warn me to leave because she cared deeply for me. I took her warning as a message from the gods. The moment I got back to the camp, I ordered that we dismantle the tents and move. My men were overjoyed. I think they were relieved they would no longer have to hear that terrifying lament at night.'

8

# WHEN THE PAINTINGS SPOKE

The prince stopped his narration suddenly, and asked, 'Do you hear footsteps?'

The two friends, who had been listening intently to his story, shook their heads and said they hadn't.

Azhvarkadiyaan thought for some time and then said, 'It suddenly seems a little warmer where we're sitting, doesn't it?'

'I can smell smoke too,' Vandiyadevan said.

'Aiya? There is no danger here, is there?' Azhvarkadiyaan asked anxiously.

'If there is any danger at all, Kaveri Amman will warn us. There's no need for worry,' the prince said, and went on, '... so, we dismantled the camp and cleared out of that place right away. Even so, ten of our soldiers fell terribly ill. Ammamma! That was a devastating illness. It would turn the most courageous of men into snivelling cowards. Those who stood strong and bore wounds on every inch of their bodies in the battlefield would find themselves so demoralised and debilitated by a sickness that lasts three days that they would beg to be allowed to return home. I believed it was the Chozha clan deity, Durga Parameshwari, who arrived in the form of that mute woman and made us leave from that place.

'Even after that incident, the goddess continued to watch over me. She has followed me everywhere I have gone. Wild animals, poisonous snakes, hidden enemies ... she has saved me from them all. She disappears as quietly as she arrives. Within days, I learnt to communicate with her through facial expressions and bodily gestures. Sometimes, it is as though my heart perceives whatever is on her mind with no need for articulation. And that's not all. Even without seeing her, I can sense when she is around. Actually, at this very moment ... right, both of you head to bed right away. Even if you're not able to sleep, pretend you're asleep. Quick!' the prince said.

They did as he bade them do. They tried to close their eyes too. But such was their curiosity that their eyelids refused to obey them.

They watched as a figure approached the latticed window through which the moonlight filtered into the room. She was the same woman whom they had seen earlier on the street, by the mansion that had caved in. A barely audible hiss escaped her lips. Arulmozhi Varmar stood up and went to the window. The woman outside made a series of signs.

The prince pointed at the two of them, his friends who lay pretending to sleep. The woman responded with more gestures.

The prince walked up to them right away and asked them to come with him. The three men left the building and followed the elderly woman.

They walked for a long time along a path flanked by tall trees that allowed little light in. All of a sudden, they arrived at a clearing and came upon a stunning sight. Several enormous elephants stood in a row, guarding a massive stupa.

Vandiyadevan's heart stopped.

The elderly woman showed no hesitation as she walked up to the herd.

Azhvarkadiyaan whispered, 'How life-like those statues look!'

It was only then that Vandiyadevan's fear abated. His wonder, however, did not.

As they came closer, they saw that the elephants had been sculpted in a phalanx, positioned as if they were bearing the weight of the stupa. Each of them had two massive tusks. There were hundreds of such elephants, across the length and breadth of the stupa. One alone appeared to have a broken tusk, and it was this elephant that the woman approached.

She moved a large stone lying by the feet of the elephant, and they could see a stairway. She disappeared down the steps, and they followed. They hadn't gone far when they came upon a mandapam lit by two oil lamps.

The woman teased the flame on one of the lamps to brighten it, and then held it up. She signalled to the prince that he alone must follow her. The other two men found this worrying at first. But once they saw that the woman was showing the prince a series of paintings on the walls of the mandapam, their anxiety for his safety lessened.

The paintings seemed to be a series of sketches that illustrated the key incidents in a story. They were of the same style as the stories of the Buddha that decorated the walls of the various viharas. But there were no images of the Buddha in these paintings. These seemed to tell the story of a woman, whose face was a younger version of the lady who now held a lamp to them. The prince realised she had illustrated her own life history on these walls.

*The first vignette was of the young woman standing all alone on the shore of a little island as her father brought back a catch of fish on his catamaran.*

*In the next picture, the woman walked through the forest.*

*Sitting on the branch of a tree was a young man, with the appearance of a prince. A bear was climbing the same tree, unnoticed by the young man, who was staring into the distance.*

*The woman screamed as she ran.*

*The bear began to chase the woman.*

*The young man jumped off the tree, aiming a spear.*

*He hurled the spear at the bear.*

*He then engaged in a duel with the bear.*

*The woman watched, leaning against a coconut tree.*

*At last, the bear collapsed in defeat.*

*The young man approached the woman.*

*He thanked her.*

*Unable to respond, the woman's eyes glistened with tears.*

*She ran to fetch her father.*

*The father arrived along with her to tell the young man that she was mute.*

*The prince looked sorrowful.*

*Then, his sorrow dissipated as the two of them became close friends.*

*The prince made a garland of wild flowers, which he gently placed around her neck as she smiled shyly.*

*The couple wandered the forest, holding hands.*

*One fine day, an enormous ship approached the island.*

*Several soldiers disembarked.*

*The soldiers found the prince and saluted him.*

*They asked him to accompany them on board the ship.*

*The prince went up to the young woman, reassured her and then left.*

*He boarded the ship.*

*The woman ached for him, and sobbed inconsolably in his absence.*

*Her father observed this.*

*He readied a boat, asked her to climb aboard and set sail.*

*They arrived at a lighthouse, where they were welcomed by a family.*

*The entire group boarded a bullock cart.*

*They went on a long journey.*

*They arrived at a city, with huge fortress walls guarding its entrance.*

*On one of the highest balconies was the prince, now wearing a crown as he waved to the crowd below. He was surrounded by soldiers in grand livery and friends and family in royal finery.*

*The young woman wilted as she saw this.*

*She ran away from the place at great speed.*

*She arrived at the lighthouse.*

*She climbed to its highest level.*

*She then jumped off, right into the sea.*

*The waves carried her limp body.*

*A man on a boat saw her.*

*He jumped off the boat.*

*He carried her unconscious body on to his boat and revived her, saving her life.*

*Assuming she had been possessed by spirits, he left her at a temple.*

*The temple priest performed a ritual, smearing vibhuti on her and hitting her with neem leaves to ward off the spirits.*

*A grand queen of some sort, who commanded everyone's obeisance, arrived at the temple for a darshan.*

*The temple priest told the queen about the mute woman.*

*The queen was pregnant at the time. She learnt that the mute woman, too, was.*

*She had her escorted into the royal palanquin and took her back to the palace with her.*

*The woman gave birth to twins in the palace garden.*

*The queen arrived and said she would raise one of the twins.*

*At first, the woman refused.*

*After giving it some thought, though, she decided it would be best for both children to be raised in the palace.*

*Leaving her newborn babies behind, she slipped away in the darkness, without telling a soul of her intentions.*

*She spent a very long time wandering the forest.*

*However, she ached to see her children every now and again.*

*She would hide among the thickets of trees by the riverbank.*

*The king, queen and children would go boating on the river often.*

*The woman would glimpse them from a distance, drink in the sight and leave.*

*Once, one of the children fell off the boat.*

*No one seemed to notice.*

*The woman waded into the water.*

*She saved the child and handed him over to his family. Then, she plunged back into the waters and swam ashore, where she disappeared among the trees.*

All these paintings, made with saffron dye, were startlingly accurate in their depiction of objects and people. Prince Arulmozhi Varmar studied each, as eager as he was astonished.

At the final painting, he turned to the woman and gestured: *I am the boy who fell into the river. You are the woman who saved my life.*

The woman, eyes brimming with tears, embraced the prince and kissed the top of his head.

She then ushered him to another corner of the mandapam, and pointed out another series of paintings. These were not incidents from her life. She used these pictures as aids, along with her gestures, to warn the prince of the various dangers that lay in his path.

Vandiyadevan and Azhvarkadiyaan had been observing the events from the spot where they were standing. The former felt more than once that the elderly woman's face bore an uncanny resemblance to Nandini's. Turbulent thoughts rose in his mind, as did several doubts. But this was not the right time to give voice to either.

Finally, the woman led them all out of the stupa and then began to climb to its top. Her flexibility amazed the three men. Vandiyadevan was exhausted from the effort, but persisted in climbing.

At the halfway point, they stopped and looked towards the city. Part of it was ablaze.

'Aha! The former palace of Mahasena Chakravarti is on fire!' the prince said.

'The place where we were sleeping?' asked Vandiyadevan.

'Yes, the very same!'

'If we had been asleep in there ...?'

'We would have been Agni Bhagavan's next meal!'

'How can you tell from such a distance that it is the very palace where we were staying?'

'From the pictures that spoke to me inside the mandapam.'

'We didn't hear what they said.'

'That is no surprise. Paintings have their own language. It makes sense only to those who can understand that language.'

'What else did the paintings tell you?'

'Several secrets that my family has been harbouring. The paintings also asked me to leave this island right away.'

'May the language of those paintings flourish forever! Vaishnavare! My side has won!' Vandiyadevan said.

'Ilavarase! That is not all the paintings said. They said you must not sleep under a roof for as long as you are in Lanka. You must not pass close to houses or under trees. Isn't that right?' Azhvarkadiyaan asked.

'You're absolutely correct. How did you know?'

'You know the language of paintings. And I know the language of gestures. When your clan deity was speaking to you, I observed her facial expressions and the signs she made,' Azhvarkadiyaan said.

'Well, good for you. There's barely one jaamam left for daybreak. Let us sleep on the roof of this stupa for some time before we leave,' Arulmozhi Varmar said.

The next morning, the rays of the sun slapped Vandiyadevan awake at dawn. As if the events of the night had not been enough, arsonists and mute people and deaf people and bears that climbed trees and ghosts and Buddhist monks and bejewelled crowns had populated Vandiyadevan's dreams in a confused story that quickly lost its plot. Those images disappeared as he opened his eyes to the sun, leaving behind fear and uncertainty.

Vandiyadevan saw that the prince and Azhvarkadiyaan had already woken up and were ready for the journey ahead. He hurried himself along, and the three men began their descent from the stupa.

They kept to the main roads as they wended their way towards the Mahamegha garden, at the centre of which stood the sacred Bodhi tree, a millennium and a half old.

Buddhist monks and devotees clustered together by the tree, doing perambulations around it and praying before it. Some had brought floral offerings. The prince bowed before the tree.

'Empires and emperors will vanish as they arrived. But this Bodhi tree stands testimony to the fact that dharma will always remain victorious and survive everything,' the prince said to his companions.

Even as he spoke, he looked about himself, observing everything. In one corner of the garden stood three horses with their grooms, ready for a journey.

The prince approached them and the three grooms broke into smiles of joy as they bowed low to greet him. The prince appeared to ask them a question. He then called to Vandiyadevan, 'It was indeed Mahasena's palace that was set on fire last night. These men were worried we had been killed. Their joy and relief on seeing us alive is quite uncontained!'

'It's true that the Bodhi tree has stood for one thousand and five hundred years. But dharma died a long time ago,' Vandiyadevan said to Azhvarkadiyaan.

'Don't ever say that again. For as long as I am alive, how can dharma possibly die?' the Vaishnavite replied.

The three men mounted the horses. They left the city of Anuradhapuram through the northern gate. The crowd that had gathered for the celebrations still teemed about, chanting and cheering, and so, no one took notice of them.

About a kaadham to the northeast of Anuradhapuram was a town called Mahindalai.

'Emperor Ashoka's son Mahinda first set foot in this town, when he came here to spread Buddhism. How lucky he was. He didn't arrive at these shores to conquer, with an army and armoury. He didn't have to run and hide from men out to murder him by night either,' Arulmozhi Varmar said.

'What a horribly boring life he must have led,' Vandiyadevan said.

The prince laughed. 'You must never leave my side. When you're around, I can find moments of cheer even in hazard.'

'And moments of cheer quickly turn into hazard,' Azhvarkadiyaan said.

At that moment, a cloud of dust rose in the distance. They could hear the sound of hooves. Soon enough, they saw a band of horsemen approaching, their spears glinting in the morning sunlight.

'Aiya! Pull your sword out of its scabbard!' Vandiyadevan warned.

# 9

## 'HERE'S YOUR WAR!'

The moment Vandiyadevan said, 'Pull your sword out of its scabbard!', the prince said, 'Right away!' and drew out his sword. Vandiyadevan had drawn out his own too.

These were monstrous weapons, terrifying in size and sharpness. The men who had met the prince's party by the Bodhi tree that morning had brought them along.

The prince now jumped off his horse and shouted, 'You! Get down here! I can no longer tolerate your presumptuousness! We're going to have it out here!'

Vandiyadevan stared at him, stunned. Why was the prince talking to him like this, he wondered. Was this a game? Or was the prince serious? But the prince had already got off his steed, and the soldier had little choice but to dismount too.

'What is the matter? Why do you hesitate? Didn't you insult me last night? Didn't you tell me my ancestors stood waiting at the door of your forebears' palace? Didn't you claim they chafed and fumed as the poets made away with their tributes? The more I think about it, the angrier I get! I can't bear this anymore. It's you or me from here on out!' the prince cried. With this, he took his sword in both arms, swung it powerfully so the blade whirled round and round, and strode towards Vandiyadevan.

Yes, dear reader, we did describe these swords as monstrous. It was no mean feat to even hold the sword with one hand. A warrior would need two hands to wield it and attack his enemy.

To watch the prince approach, swinging the sword, one wouldn't think he had grown up in the lap of luxury in a palace, amid the tender care of the women residing in the palace antapuram. One would think he had been schooled in warfare all his life. He could be Bhima or Arjuna or Abhimanyu, walking through the battlefield at Kurukshetra. He could be Vijayalaya Chozhar, who had carried six and ninety scars on his hallowed body. He could be Rajaditya Chozhar, who had ridden his war elephant to the heavens. He was their rightful heir. He had their regal bearing and peerless courage.

Vandiyadevan swung his own sword with both arms too. The confusion and hesitation that had stalled him disappeared. His mind was clear. His heart was steady. He forgot that his opponent was his beloved prince, the man he had come to admire so much from such a short acquaintance. He forgot that he had been wondering what the prince's intentions were. He forgot that he didn't know why they were engaging in a duel. All he could see was the enemy's sword. All he could think was that he must ensure that the sword did not hurt him, and that he must find a way to disarm his opponent and pin him down.

The rhythm of the swords slicing through the air and clashing against each other with a 'danaar, danaar' went from the vilambha kaalam to the madhyama kaalam to the druta kaalam.[1]

At first, Azhvarkadiyaan hadn't understood what the prince was up to either. But he figured there must be some strong motive for this bizarre challenge. Perhaps the prince had come up with a strategy to halt the horsemen who were headed their way, to figure out who they were and then determine his own course of action accordingly. And so, Azhvarkadiyaan busied himself with reining in the horses of the two duellers, and guiding them to the side of the road along with his own.

The horsemen whom they had heard approaching were closer now. Azhvarkadiyaan could now make out a tiger flag held aloft. His worries dissipated. They were Chozha warriors. But who could they be?

The mystery was solved by the criers who preceded the party with their drums.

'The vanquisher of Mahinda in the Lankan war, the senapati of the army that drove him off the battlefield, the man who beheaded Veerapandiyan[2] in the Vaigaiyaatru battle, Kodumbalur Periya Velaar Boothi Vikrama Kesari Maharaja is headed this way. Paraak! Paraak!' they announced.

'The scion of the Pallava clan, the bravest of brave warriors who beheaded Veerapandiyan[3], he who defeated the Vengi armies in the Vadapennai war, Parthibendra Varmar is headed this way. Paraak! Paraak!' another group of criers announced.

A group of about thirty horsemen followed the criers. In their midst, riding the most majestic of white stallions, were Boothi Vikrama Kesari and Parthibendran. Bringing up the rear of the party was an enormous elephant bearing a howdah.

In the distance, blurred by the dust the horses had raised, was an infantry regiment.

The cavalrymen were none too pleased at finding their path blocked by a duel.

'Who goes there?' one of the horsemen cried.

'Out of the way!'

'Clear the path!'

Then, there were some murmurs among the men up front. Gasps and exclamations of surprise susurrused their way through the group.

The men now dismounted and surrounded the two fighters.

Boothi Vikrama Kesari and Parthibendran, too, dismounted and made their way to the forefront.

Parthibendran was in a tizzy. He turned to the senapati and said, 'Do you see now? What did I say about that Vandiyadevan? Do you see I was right? Look at him now! Arrogant rascal! You see his presumptuousness? He dares challenge the prince himself! Are we to watch on in silence?' With this, he unsheathed his sword.

Boothi Vikrama Kesari arrested his arm. 'Hold on! What a stunning duel! How long it has been since I watched something of this quality!'

The infantry regiment, comprising about three hundred warriors, had joined them by now. They formed a phalanx around the duellers and watched.

A young woman had silently slipped down from the howdah the elephant carried. She wove her way through the soldiers until she reached the innermost circle of the audience.

We must go to some effort now to describe the agitation of this woman. As the swords flew through the air, her eyeballs danced the same arc. Her waist moved in time with the two men as they pranced their way around each other. She reached for the neelotpala flower she had tucked into her hair and imitated the swirls of the swords.

The readers need hardly be told who this young woman was. Yes. You couldn't have forgotten Poonguzhali, could you?

At first, the prince was facing her. As the duel went on and the two men wound their way through a half-circle, she could see them in profile. Then, Vandiyadevan's face came into view.

Vandiyadevan saw from the corner of his eye that the audience was growing. Suddenly, he spotted Poonguzhali's face in the crowd. His astonishment distracted him for a moment, and that was enough for the prince. Arulmozhi Varmar brought down his sword like Indra's Vajrayudha and sent Vandiyadevan's weapon clattering to the ground.

As the Vaanar scion staggered back, the audience broke into applause and cheers that could have drowned out the ocean. A young woman's laughter broke through the men's cries.

Vandiyadevan lunged to retrieve his sword, but the prince stepped in his way and embraced him.

'You didn't lose to my sword,' he said. 'You matched me stroke for stroke. But then, you lost to a different kind of blade—a woman's weapon, her eyes. There is no shame in that. It happens to everyone.'

Before Vandiyadevan could respond, the senapati and Parthibendran were upon them.

'Ilavarase! It was I who sent this boy to you. Has he erred in some way? We were shaken by the sight!' the senapati said.

'Yes, Commander! I cannot brook his badgering. He went on and on and on. "You said there's a war on in Lanka? Where is the war? Where's the war? They told me a war was being fought here! I don't see war!" I couldn't take it anymore. I said, "Here's your war!" and showed him.'

At the prince's words, another round of cheers broke out.

The senapati went up to Vandiyadevan and patted his back. 'Appane!' he said, 'Do you know how long it's been since I saw a duel like this? You're the perfect companion for the prince! Every now and again, his shoulders itch to swing the sword, you see. He is, after all, born into the lineage of Parantaka Chakravarti who is known as "Kunjaramallan"[4]! One can't sustain a friendship with him for long unless one is capable of duelling with him every now and again!'

By this time, the prince had gone up to Parthibendra Pallavar and said, 'Aiya! I heard that you had come all the way from Kanchi to Anuradhapuram in search of me. I've hurried along for the express purpose of meeting you. Is my brother well? How is my grandfather?'

'Your brother and grandfather have sent a crucial message for you. I've already squandered several days in Lanka, trying to find you. There isn't a moment left to lose ...' Parthibendran began, when the prince interrupted him.

'If the message were not crucial, would they have sent as grand a messenger as you?' Ponniyin Selvar said. 'We needn't lose another moment. Do give me their message right away.'

The senapati walked up to them and said, 'This is not a discussion we ought to be having in the middle of the road, with so many onlookers. There, I see a mandapam. Let's go there. Thankfully, there is no shortage of dilapidated mandapams in Lanka!'

The party made for the mandapam.

10

A CONFERENCE

As they headed for the mandapam, Vandiyadevan moved closer to Azhvarkadiyaan and said, 'What do I make of the prince's actions now? The other day, he took me on in a fistfight. Today, he started a swordfight. Would it kill him to give me a heads-up before jumping into a duel? Friendship with the prince appears to be fraught with danger!'

The prince, who was also moving towards the two, heard his words.

'That's true, aiya ... friendship with me *is* fraught with danger. Wasn't last night enough evidence of this fact? If you want to safeguard yourself from danger, you'll have to put at least ten kaadhams between the two of us.'

'That wasn't my complaint, Your Highness. I'm happy to stand by your side and face any danger we might encounter. It is these sudden duels in which I'm made an unwilling, involuntary opponent that I ...'

Azhvarkadiyaan interrupted with, 'Thambi, haven't you understood why the prince resorts to this? It is simply to buy time to figure out who the approaching party is, and tailor his demeanour accordingly. Whoever that may be, a fight will make them stop and watch for a while, won't it?'

'Tirumalai is right,' the prince said. 'And there's another thing. My horoscope says that anyone who becomes a friend of mine will be subject to the jealousy and hatred and enmity of everyone else. And so, anyone whom I wish to befriend must be subjected to duels every so often. It is only those who are happy to acquiesce in this who qualify for friendship with me, I'm afraid.'

'Well, if that's the case, so be it. I won't wait for you to start the next fight. I'll do the honours myself. Ilavarase! I, who was sent as your messenger, have forgotten to pass on an important message. Let me tell you now. I absolutely must. If you don't wish to listen, do take up your sword again!' Vandiyadevan said.

'No, no, there's no need for that ... please give me this important message, I'm listening.'

'Do you remember earlier, in the crowd standing around us, there was a girl with a flower in her hand? You told me I'd lost to a woman's weapon, her eyes, didn't you? Do you know who that girl is?'

'I don't. I didn't really get a good look at her. It's not in my nature to stare at women.'

'Ilavarase! She's the one who wanted me to pass on that important message. And I forgot to deliver it. What can I say, between duelling with you and running for my life I didn't quite find the right opportunity to speak to you about her. It was only when I saw her that I remembered I'd forgotten to carry out her request. And it was at this moment of remembrance that you knocked the sword out of my hands.'

'Well, that's all in the past. Who is that woman? And why does she seek to send me a message?'

'Aiya! She is Poonguzhali.'

'That is a beautiful name. But it doesn't ring a bell.'

'Aiya! Do you remember the name "Samudra Kumari"?'

'Samudra Kumari ... Samudra Kumari ... I'm afraid I don't. I don't recall ever seeing that girl either.'

'Please jog your memory. If I were to tell that girl you have no recollection of her, her heart would break into pieces. In Kodikkarai, you were looking for a boat to take you to the warship. You saw a girl row a boat by herself and draw it ashore. You looked on in surprise. She was curious about who you and your entourage were, and she approached you. You then asked the lighthouse keeper who this girl was. He told you she was his daughter. At that point, you said to him, "Your daughter, really? I thought she was the daughter of the ocean, Samudra Kumari!" That girl has never forgotten those words. It is only because of her that I was able to cross the ocean and reach Lanka.'

'Now that you say it, I seem to recall an incident of the sort. But what is Samudra Kumari from Kodikkarai doing here in Anuradhapuram? Why has she accompanied these men here? Was it in search of you, perhaps?'

'No, there's no way that could happen. There is no reason for her to search for me. If she's here in search of someone, it must be you. Don't ask me why, though … I have no idea.'

Even as he said this, Vandiyadevan glanced at Poonguzhali, who was walking by the senapati's side some distance away. She was keeping her head low, staring modestly at the ground. However, he sensed that her thoughts and attention were entirely on the prince. Every now and again, she would cast a sideways glance at Ponniyin Selvan. She must have sensed that they were talking about her. That was the only reason she would put on this docile act. Ammamma! Those lovely, lively eyes of hers were incapable of looking steadfastly at the ground without supreme effort.

They now reached a mandapam whose roof had fallen in. Only ornate pillars of black stone remained standing as testament to its past glory. The trees around the mandapam formed something of a canopy and provided shelter from the heat. There was a raised platform inside the mandapam, and the prince, the senapati and Parthibendran seated themselves on it. Vandiyadevan and Azhvarkadiyaan stood some distance away. Poonguzhali hid behind a pillar, with a vantage view of the prince and Vandiyadevan.

The soldiers assembled in two rows, as if in formation, around the mandapam. The horses and elephants stood further away.

The prince turned to Parthibendran and asked, 'What message have my brother and grandfather sent? I'm keen to hear.'

'Ilavarase! There is great peril facing the Chozha kingdom. You must be aware of this yourself.'

'True, aiya, the emperor has been ill for a long time.'

'That is not the only peril. The very empire is in danger. Men with much influence have turned traitors. They're conspiring against the emperor, the crown prince and you. They claim that your brother is not the rightful heir. They want to crown as prince that man who pretends to be a Shiva bhaktan, that rudraksha poonai[1] Madurantakan. The Pazhuvettaraiyar brothers, Sambuvarayar and his son, the kings of Irattai Kudai, Mazhapadi Mazhuvarayar and several other powerful suzerains have joined this group. But there is no need for us to panic. We have the strength of the northern and southern forces. Tirukkovalur Miladudaiyar and Kodumbalur Periya Velaar are with us. With their counsel and our armies, we will decimate our enemies in no time at all. But we must not delay action. We must nip their conspiracy in the bud. It is to plan for this that your brother and grandfather have asked me to escort you to Kanchi right away. Your grandfather feels it is critical that you brothers be in the same spot, and not be separated. I also wish to tell you how your brother feels. He has little interest in staying put in the capital and ruling the empire. He wishes to conquer territories across the ocean and ensure that the Chozha flag flies across the world. He itches for war. Since the Pazhuvettaraiyar brothers have put a stop to our voyages of conquest in the north, his hunger for battle has only grown … grown five times, ten times. All he wants is for you to come to Kanchi, so that the two of you can march to Thanjavur and put paid to your enemies there. He will then crown you heir and set off on his …'

The prince, who had been listening patiently all this while, now clapped his ears shut with his hands and cried, 'No, no! Stop! Don't speak such terrible words! I want nothing to do with the Chozha throne.'

'If you don't wish to hear the words, I will not speak them. This is between you and your brother. The two of you must decide that course of action. But it is critical that you both stay united in your wish to destroy your enemies. We will uproot the Pazhuvettaraiyars and Sambuvarayars. We will send Madurantakan to his beloved Shivalokam. And then, your brother and you can figure out who will sit on the throne after your father,' Parthibendran said.

'Aiya! Is it all up to the two of us to decide? Shouldn't we ask our father, the emperor, what *his* wishes are? Or, do you know what he wants us to do? Has he passed on any confidential messages to my brother?'

'Ilavarase! Under such circumstances, I must speak the truth. There is little point in hiding it. It is impossible for us to know what your father's wishes truly are. He is not a free man. The Pazhuvettaraiyar brothers have imprisoned him. No one can meet the emperor without their permission. How are we then to divine his wishes? Your brother has undertaken enormous efforts to free your father from their clutches and bring him to the safety of Kanchi. He has even built a golden palace. He invited your father to come to the palace and inaugurate it. But we have received no response from the emperor.'

'But we already know that my father is ill and cannot walk.'

'Ilavarase! Must your father—the emperor of the three worlds—walk to Kanchi? Are there no horses and elephants to carry him? Are there no chariots inside which he can lie down comfortably and travel to Kanchi? Won't the suzerain kings who remain loyal to him fight each other for the chance to carry him on their own shoulders all the way to Kanchi? His illness is not what precludes a visit. It is the Pazhuvettaraiyar brothers' treachery that does. The Thanjai palace has now turned into the emperor's prison. Ilavarase! If you wish to save your father's life, you must leave with me right away!'

The effect of these words on the prince was obvious. His face clouded over with worry. After some minutes of silent contemplation, the prince turned to the senapati and asked, 'Senapati, what do you think? Some days ago, the prime minister spoke to me. He told me he felt I should remain in Lanka for some time. You agreed with him. When I asked you what work I had here when we will not have a chance to wage war for months, you convinced me to stay. The prime minister has reiterated his opinion to our Vaishnavite friend. My sister, for whom you know I have the highest esteem, has sent me instructions to leave for Pazhaiyarai right away. And my brother has asked me to come to Kanchi. Senapati! What is your opinion?'

'Ilavarase! Until this morning, I was sure the right course of action was for you to remain in Lanka. I was, in fact, debating this point well into the night with Parthibendra Pallavar. I remained unconvinced by his arguments. But this morning, the girl you see there brought me some news, which prompted me to change my mind. Now, I feel you must leave for Kanchi right away,' the senapati said.

The prince now turned to Poonguzhali, who was looking at him from behind the pillar. He said, 'You must have heard the story of Abhimanyu being swarmed by his enemies from all four sides and getting killed. It appears I will be swarmed by instructions from all four sides and get killed. What is this news that made you change your mind?'

'Let her tell you herself,' the senapati said.

Poonguzhali walked forward hesitantly. She stood before the prince, and looked about herself. She looked at the senapati, and she looked at Parthibendran. She looked at Vandiyadevan and Azhvarkadiyaan. But she wasn't able to look at the prince.

'Penne, out with it now, quick!' the senapati said.

Poonguzhali opened her mouth to say something. But no words came forth.

'Aha! It appears the entire world has gone mute!' Arulmozhi Varmar said.

At this, Poonguzhali jerked her head up and met the prince's gaze. And then, tears began to pour out of her eyes. She turned tail and ran. She ran until the edge of the clearing and then disappeared into the trees.

Everyone looked on, stunned.

Vandiyadevan stepped forward and said, 'Aiya! She has done this before. I'll run after her and bring her back.'

'Do as you say, but first, let the senapati tell me what news she brought!' the prince said.

'That will only take a minute,' the senapati said. 'Ilavarase! The Pazhuvettaraiyar brothers have sent two huge ships full of soldiers to arrest you. They are now hidden away in a lagoon by the river Thondaimanaru.'

## 11

## 'LOOK, OVER THERE!'

The prince broke into a smile upon hearing the senapati's words.

'It appears the conflict raging within my heart has finally reached a resolution,' he mumbled, almost to himself.

Parthibendran rose, fuming.

'Senapati! What did you just say? Is this true? Why did you hide this from me all along? It is only now that I see why you brought that insane girl along! I ask again—is it really true that the Pazhuvettaraiyar brothers have sent ships to arrest the prince?'

'Yes, aiya. If we are to believe what that girl claims she saw with her own eyes and heard with her own ears.'

'Aha! That old man Tirukkovalur Milaadudaiyar was right after all. He knows how the Pazhuvettaraiyars think. Senapati! What else are you waiting for? The Pazhuvettaraiyar brothers, of all people, dare send men to arrest the scion of Parantaka Chakravarti's clan, the prince who is beloved of the people, the apple of everyone's eye, the brother of Aditya Karikalar, Arulmozhi Varmar? What temerity! How much more will it take to jolt you into action? We will leave with our armies right away and bury every single man who has come to arrest our prince on this very island. And then we can put the plan we have already made into action. Come, let us leave! What are we waiting for?' Parthibendran spluttered.

Senapati Boothi Vikrama Kesari turned to him and said, 'Parthibendra! It was precisely because I knew you would react like this that I kept it from you. This calls for contemplation. We must give it some thought and decide what to do next. We can't simply jump into action.'

'Thought? What thought? And why? You think this is a time for contemplation? Ilavarase! Tell me yourself ... what *is* there that merits "giving it some thought"? Even if you had cause to wait earlier, what could possibly delay action now? We must uproot the Pazhuvettaraiyars, every single member of that clan!'

At this, the prince said, 'Let's find out what the senapati has in mind, perhaps? Aiya! What is the issue to which you feel we must give some thought?' He spoke in a steady tone, with no nervous energy or anger.

'If the people who have come to arrest you ... it stings my tongue to even speak those words, but I'm afraid I must speak them ... well, if they are here to arrest you on the emperor's orders, what do we do? Do we take up arms against them even in that case?'

Parthibendran guffawed. 'What an idea!' he said. 'Is the emperor in any condition to issue orders? The Pazhuvettaraiyar brothers have imprisoned him, haven't they?'

Vandiyadevan entered the fray with, 'The Pallava commander is right. I saw for myself. The emperor has all but been imprisoned by the Pazhuvettaraiyar brothers. No one can meet the emperor unless they allow it; no one can speak to him without their consent. All I did was utter a single word, and they went after me with such force! My arm still hurts where Chinna Pazhuvettaraiyar grasped it.' He massaged his wrist.

'Well said, Vallavaraya! I was wrong about you, it appears. Tell the prince and senapati again what you just said, say it so they understand what they're dealing with!' Parthibendran cried.

'There is no need for that, he has said all he needs to say,' the prince said, and then turned to Vandiyadevan. 'Aiya! You said you would run after that girl and bring her back. Why are you still here? Let's hear her account in full detail. She seems to be rather ... odd. Do you think you could talk her into coming back here somehow?'

'I'll leave right away, Ilavarase! I'll bring her back with me. I cannot bear the thought of your being imprisoned by the Pazhuvettaraiyars. For as long as there is breath in my body, I will not allow it to happen,' Vandiyadevan said.

'Senapati, you are yet to give us your opinion,' Arulmozhi Varmar said, as Vandiyadevan took off.

'Well, this is my opinion—you must not meet the men who have come to arrest you. You should leave for Kanchi on the ship Parthibendran has brought right away. I will head to Thanjavur. I will meet the emperor in person, and find out what exactly is going on.'

'For you to go to Thanjavur is to stick your head in the lion's den, senapati. You will not return. You will be thrown into the dungeon. You cannot meet the emperor,' Parthibendran said.

'What nonsense! Which man in Chozha Naadu dares throw me into a dungeon? Which man dares prevent me from meeting the emperor? Besides, Prime Minister Aniruddha Brahmarayar will be there, and ...'

'True, Brahmarayar will be there. So? He's not able to meet the emperor himself. Here, his shishya is right here. Why don't we ask his opinion?'

The senapati turned to Azhvarkadiyaan and said, 'Ah, I forgot all about our Veera Vaishnavan. Tirumalai! Don't you have anything to say? Or has, as the prince said, the entire world gone mute?'

'Senapati! God has given us two ears and only one mouth. My guru taught me that the point of this is to keep one's ears open to the extent possible and mouth closed to the extent possible. He said this was particularly important when grand, important matters concerning the kingdom were being discussed.'

'Well, you have imbibed your guru's words well. Now, answer because I ask—what is your opinion?'

'On what, senapati?'

'On what we have been discussing all this while. What do you think the prince should do? Stay on in Lanka? Or go to Kanchi?'

'Do you want my honest opinion? If the prince permits me, I'll tell you.'

Arulmozhi Varmar, who appeared lost in thought, came to at his words and said, 'Yes, Tirumalai, you have my permission. Do tell us what you have in mind.'

'We must look for the highest security prison in Lanka and lock the prince up inside. And then we should beef up the security outside even further.'

'What is he on about?' the senapati asked.

'Is this the time for clowning around?' Parthibendran demanded.

'I'm not clowning around. I'm telling you what I think. Yesterday, the prince was walking the streets of Anuradhapuram. A building nearly came crashing down on his head. Not long after, the palace in which we were staying was set on fire. Thankfully, we had stepped out for a bit. Ask the prince yourselves whether this is true or not.'

The two men turned to the prince. His expression confirmed Azhvarkadiyaan's account.

'And who do you think their target was? Would someone set a house on fire to kill me or Vandiyadevan?'

Parthibendran leapt up and said, 'Someone is trying to assassinate the prince! What further proof do we need that he is unsafe? This is all the more reason he must accompany me to Kanchi!'

'Never! It would be a better idea to hand the prince over to the Pazhuvettaraiyar brothers than to send him with you,' Azhvarkadiyaan said.

'Vaishnavane! How dare you!' Parthibendran fumed, reaching for his sword.

The senapati stopped him, and said, 'Tirumalai! What makes you speak these words? Don't you know just how loyal Parthibendra Pallavar is to the Chozha dynasty?'

'I know, senapati, I know. But is one's friendship and fealty enough?'

'I know that Parthibendrar would sacrifice his life to honour his friendships, Tirumalai!'

'That's as may be. But let him answer this question—when we were nearing Thamballai the day before yesterday, we saw two men accompany him. Who were those men and where are they now? Can he tell me?'

Parthibendra Pallavan looked startled for a moment. He then responded, somewhat hesitantly, 'I met them at Tirikonamalai. They told me they would escort me to the prince. Then, they disappeared into thin air in

Anuradhapuram. Why do you ask, Vaishnavane? Do you know something about those men?'

'Yes, I do. I know that the two of them are part of a group that has sworn to destroy the Chozha dynasty. I think it was they who tried to assassinate the prince in Anuradhapuram yesterday. Aha! Look, over there!' Azhvarkadiyaan suddenly interrupted himself and pointed at something.

They all turned towards the direction in which he was pointing. Among the thick foliage, they could make out the form of a lovely girl and a well-built youth. It appeared Vandiyadevan's mission had been successful, and he was walking back with Poonguzhali. All of a sudden, the man reached for the woman's dagger and flung it at a bush they were passing.[1] A scream rose from the bush.

# 12

## POONGUZHALI'S DAGGER

Vandiyadevan had set off in search of Poonguzhali, only to find her leaning against a tree right at the edge of the clearing, sobbing softly.

He called, in as gentle a voice as he could, 'Poonguzhali!'

The sound startled her, and she whipped her head around.

'Oh, it's you, is it?' she said, and then turned away from him.

'Yes, it is. Why are you angry with me?'

'I'm not angry with you.'

'Then why did you act as you did?'

'I don't like men at all. Not one bit.'

'Not even the prince?'

Poonguzhali turned around again and glared at him. 'Yes,' she said. 'Especially not the prince. I don't like him at all.'

'What crime has he committed to rouse such ...'

'He doesn't remember me. He didn't so much as glance at me.'

'He remembers you very well indeed. In fact, when I mentioned you, he said, "Oh, do you think I don't know Samudra Kumari?"'

'You're lying.'

'Ask him yourself.'

'If he remembered me, why didn't he utter a single word to me?'

'He did. It was you who ran away without answering him.'

'That's not what I'm talking about. When you see someone you know, don't you go up to that person and ask after her? That's how I know you're lying. Like I said, he didn't so much as glance at me.'

'Poonguzhali! There is a reason the prince is acting like that.'

'What is this reason?'

'The prince is in a precarious situation. It is a terrible time for him.'

'According to whom?'

'All the astrologers say so. The astrologer of Kudandai told me as much himself.'

'What did he tell you?'

'That the prince will face problem after problem, challenge after challenge, for some time. And so will the people close to him. Everyone who makes his acquaintance will be affected. The prince is aware of this. That is why he pushes everyone away. He doesn't want to befriend anyone. He would rather face all these problems and challenges on his own than cause someone else to suffer alongside him.'

'Why are you an exception to this rule?'

'Didn't you see him take a sword to me and try to make an enemy of me? He started the fight for no reason at all, to chase me away. It only ended because the lot of you arrived at that spot.'

'And even if he chases you away, you would refuse to go?'

'I would. I will share every one of his problems, stand by his side through every one of his challenges, and share his pain.'

'You like him so much, do you?'

'Yes, I do. Very, very much.'

'Why?'

'I'm not able to explain. The moment I laid eyes on him, I was drawn to him.'

'The same thing happened to me!' Poonguzhali said. The next moment, she bit her lip, regretting that she had opened her heart to Vandiyadevan.

'I know you like the prince. That is why I have come for you. Let's go.'

'No!' Poonguzhali said firmly.

'If you won't come of your own free will, I'll have to force you.'

'One step forward, and I'll use this on you,' Poonguzhali said, grabbing the dagger she had tucked into her waist.

'Paavi penne![1] What do you want to stab me for? For reminding the prince about you?'

'You're lying. You haven't said a word about me to the prince.'

'Fine, believe what you want to believe. Now, you said there were two ships full of men out to arrest the prince and take him back home, didn't you? Come, tell the prince what you know and then go your way. I couldn't care less!'

'I've told the senapati all that I know.'

'The prince wishes to hear it straight from you.'

'I'm struck dumb when I stand before him.'

'The prince is very fond of mute women!'

'Chhi chhi! You're making fun of me!' Poonguzhali said angrily, and aimed her dagger.

'So, you won't come with me, is it?'

'I won't!'

'Fine, I'm going then!' Vandiyadevan said, and turned back. He took two steps forward, then swung around, lunged at Poonguzhali, grabbed her dagger and flung it away.

The dagger swirled through the air and landed on a bush. A shrill cry rose from the bush. They couldn't tell whether the voice was human or animal or avian.

Poonguzhali, who had glared at Vandiyadevan with enraged eyes when he'd grabbed her knife, turned to look at the bush as soon as she heard the scream. Then, she and Vandiyadevan looked at each other. They moved stealthily towards the bush and peeked behind it. They could see fresh blood splattered on the leaves and the ground. But there wasn't a soul about. Poonguzhali's dagger was missing too.

'You see, Poonguzhali? I told you the prince was in a precarious situation, didn't I? Do you see now that he is surrounded by danger? One can't tell what might happen or when. I happened to grab the knife from you and throw it. And we got to know, serendipitously, that someone was hiding in the bush. Think ... why would someone hide here? Didn't you tell me two men had preceded me to Kodikkarai, and that your brother had rowed them here? You said you had a bad feeling about those men, that you found them repulsive. At such a time, can people who care for the prince think to abandon him?' Vandiyadevan said, all in one breath.

'What if he asks me to go?' Poonguzhali asked.

'Even if he does, we must refuse to go!'

Poonguzhali thought for a bit, and then asked, 'Shouldn't we find out who was hiding here?'

'We can't. How do we find that person in such a dense forest? If we linger here any longer, the prince will get so angry that he'll ask everyone to pack up and leave without us. Now, stop arguing and come with me.'

'Fine, I will.'

The two made their way towards the mandapam.

The party greeted them with questions.

'Why did you throw the dagger at the bush?'

 *Wind Storm*

'What was that sound we heard?'

'Whose cry was that?'

'I thought I heard an animal in the bush, perhaps a leopard or a fox. That's why I threw the dagger. We went to check right after, but there was nothing there,' Vandiyadevan said.

'Who cares about all this? Ask this girl what you wanted to!' the senapati said.

Poonguzhali had eyes only for the prince. Now, he returned her gaze.

*Chhi, chhi! Why does my heart hammer like this?* thought Poonguzhali. *My throat is dry. Why do I feel tears rising to my eyes? Idiot girl, where is your courage? Your heart which remains steadfast through sea storms and giant waves now wavers ... why? You have looked an angry tiger in the eye without fear, but you can't hold the gaze of a man? Don't earn the title of 'insane woman' yet again ... go on, look the prince in the eye! Answer him when he speaks to you. Talk to him in your loud, clear voice. What is he going to do to you, anyway? Everyone speaks of him as a compassionate and generous man ... what is he going to do to an innocent girl like you?*

'Samudra Kumari! Do you remember me?'

She heard his words as if from the bottom of the ocean.

## 13

## 'I'M GUILTY!'

'Samudra Kumari! Do you remember me?'

'Ponniyin Selva! What sort of question is this? To whom do you address such a question? "Do you remember me?" you ask! When we have spent entire millennia in each other's company, what might move you to ask such a question? Or is it that you have forgotten me? How many aeons passed as we sailed in that little boat, just the two of us? We sat floating on waves that melted into the skies, the open sea with its waters stretched as far as the eye could see meeting the vast skies to wash away all notion of time and space. Have you forgotten? Have you forgotten how, as the dusk descended around us, and as we were subsumed by the darkness, we held hands, fingers entwined? Have you forgotten how, as the waves rose and tossed us up into the skies one moment and sank us into the bowels of the earth the next, we stood together, each a pillar of support that the other could lean on?

Have you forgotten how we flew and flew and flew through the cosmos? Have you forgotten how you leapt up to catch the stars and placed them gently on my head, arranging them to ornament my hair? Have you forgotten, too, how you brought the full moon to me and said, "Look, look, don't you want to see your face in this silver mirror I have brought you?" Have you forgotten how I panicked as you dove into the sea, only to emerge with pearls and corals in either hand? Have you forgotten how you strung them together yourself, and garlanded my neck with that chain? And even if *you* have forgotten all this, how could I have? Arase! Can I possibly forget those endless afternoons we whiled away among bowers of flowers on the seashore, lost in each other's eyes? Or how hundreds of lovebirds sat on the branches over our heads and sang together? Or how thousands of bees hummed to that music? Or how millions of butterflies danced around us? Can I forget all this, in this lifetime and in the many lifetimes I am yet to live? Do I remember you, you ask? How could you? I do remember you, aiya, I remember everything about you!'

And so Poonguzhali's heart ached to speak.

However, all her lips could say was, 'Yes, I do.'

'Aha! Samudra Kumari! You have spoken! The mandapams on this wondrous island are held up by pillars carved into some of the most stunning sculptures I have seen ... sculptures of women too beautiful to truly exist. And I wondered for a moment whether you were one of those sculptures. Thankfully, you have spoken out loud. Speak some more, let me hear another phrase or two. I ache to hear that dulcet voice of yours. I believe you brought some news for the senapati? You said, I believe, that two ships full of soldiers have been anchored discreetly on the Thondaimanaru? Is this true, Samudra Kumari? Have you seen those ships with your own eyes?' the prince asked.

'Yes, aiya, I've seen them with my very own eyes,' Poonguzhali said.

'Ah! We finally hear your voice. My ears are grateful for it. You did well to row your boat into an inconspicuous canal once you saw the ships. I believe you also snuck into the forest and waited to see what the men would do next. You stayed hidden among the trees, as some of them stepped off the ship and settled down near your hiding spot. Although you hadn't intended to eavesdrop on them, you couldn't help but hear what they said. This, I believe, was your account to the senapati?'

'I told him what happened as it happened,' Poonguzhali replied.

'And the moment you heard what they said, it struck you that our senapati must be warned. When the soldiers left, you took off too. You learnt where the senapati was, and rushed to him. How did you do this, Samudra Kumari?'

'I rowed halfway, and walked the rest through the forest.'

'And how did you know where to go?'

'I figured the senapati would be at Mathottam and set off in that direction. On my way, I heard that he was at Mahindalai. It was such a mammoth effort to meet him! How many people tried to stop me!' Poonguzhali said, and then turned to glare at the senapati. Sparks flew from her eyes.

'Meeting the head of the army cannot be an easy task now, can it? If you were to hear of the travails my friend had to undergo in order to meet him, you'd be stunned. Anyway, it's a good thing you wouldn't let any obstacle stand in your way. Will you repeat before me what you told the senapati? What did the men say when they stopped near your hiding spot?'

'Arase! It would sting my tongue to repeat those words.'

'Please do it for my sake, just the once.'

'They spoke about how they were here to arrest you.'

'Did they mention on whose orders they had come?'

'I didn't believe what they said, aiya! I thought the moment I heard the words that this must be a conspiracy of the Pazhuvettaraiyars.'

'Please reserve your opinion for later, and simply tell me what exactly you heard them say, Samudra Kumari!'

'They claimed the order was issued by the emperor.'

'All right, excellent. Did they mention a reason for this?'

'Yes. They claimed you had conspired with the Buddhist monks in this kingdom and arranged to be crowned king of this island. I was so furious when I heard those creatures say this that I wanted to kill them right then and there!'

'Quite a brilliant idea. Don't you know better than to throw any kind of obstacle in the way of the emperor's messengers, let alone cause their death by your very own hands? Well ... did you hear them say anything else of significance?'

'That the senapati should not know why they were here, because he would find a way of getting you away safely. They said they must find out where you were and give you the order personally and escort you to Chozha Naadu right away.'

'And so, you headed off in search of the senapati right away. Well, this is no ordinary service, Samudra Kumari! You have been of enormous help to me. All right, now, give me a few moments. I need to consult these gentlemen on a matter of great importance. But don't run away like you did last time and force me to send Vandiyadevan in pursuit.'

Samudra Kumari moved towards a pillar which would afford her a good view of the prince's face.

Imagine two bees that had been drowning in a pot of honey. Imagine their joy as they slowly surface and can actually taste the honey without being overwhelmed by it. So it was that Poonguzhali's eyes revelled in the bliss, as they sipped the honey that was the beautifully chiselled face of the prince. Her heart, however, refused to stay captive in her chest. It ached to jump out of her ribcage and soar into the air, even if that would cause her chest to burst.

The prince turned to the senapati and said, 'Aiya! You are the head of a clan that has, for generations, been a close ally of our own. You are a close friend of my father's, and I think of you quite as a father to me. You have shown me all the love you would your own son. And so, I ask that you help me carry out my duty. You must not stand in my way!'

Before the senapati could reply, he turned to Parthibendran and said, 'Aiya! I ask of you too. You are a close friend of my elder brother's. To me, my brother's words are sacrosanct and so I'm duty-bound to treat your words the same way. I beg of you, please do not stop me from carrying out my obligations.'

The senapati and Parthibendran looked at each other. The face of each mirrored the other's fear.

The senapati turned to the prince and said, 'Ilavarase! I can't make sense of what you said. I've spent my entire life on the battlefield. Subtle speech is not my forté and hints are lost on me. You say you will carry out your obligations. What does that mean? Which obligation do you intend to carry out, and how?'

'I have only one obligation at the moment. I must obey my father's orders. The emperor has sent men to arrest me. Why must we make them set out in search of me? I will approach them myself and surrender.'

'Impossible! No, absolutely not! Not for as long as I have breath in my body! I'll never allow it. I *will* stop you!' Parthibendran said.

The senapati turned to him and said, 'There's no need to get into a panic. Hold on, let's talk it out.' He then turned to the prince and said, 'Aiya! You spoke of your own duty. But I have a duty too. I beg you to hear me out. I am the only living male heir of the Kodumbalur Velaar family. Everyone else from our dynasty died in the service of the Chozha crown. I, too, will meet that same fate one day. Who cares? So, I ask that you bear with me as I speak. Last year, the Chakravarti made you Marthanda Nayagan of the Southern front—you, the darling of the palace, you, who have grown up knowing nothing but comfort. Afterwards, he had a private conversation with me. He said: "My impending separation from the prince fills me with dread. It is as good as my soul being separated from my body. But I'm aware that I cannot force him to remain inside the palace forever simply because I wish to keep him by my side. He must go to the battle-front. He must win wars, and earn the title of hero as his brother has. But if there is the slightest danger to his life, your life is at stake too. It is your responsibility to ensure he is safe at all times. On pain of death." These were the emperor's orders. Can you imagine that your father, who spoke these words last year, would possibly order you arrested this week? What have you done to merit such an order? What a travesty of the truth it is to accuse you of conspiring to seize the Lankan throne! Would anyone believe such a thing?'

The prince, who had been listening patiently thus far, interjected at this point, 'I'm not sure whether anyone else would believe it, but I certainly can!'

'What are you saying, ilavarase?'

'I'm saying it is indeed true that I conspired to seize the Lankan throne.'

Vandiyadevan stepped up now and said, 'What is this, aiya! You were talking about Satya and Dharma moments ago, and now you lie through your teeth! Senapati! Please do not believe a word he says. The Mahasabha of the Buddha gurus offered him the crown and the throne of Lanka last night, and he refused both. This Vaishnavite and I were eyewitnesses.'

Ponniyin Selvar smiled and said, 'Vandiyadevare! I have a question for you. Do conspirators usually conspire with witnesses present? It could have been that the very reason I refused the crown and the throne was the presence of the two of you there, no?'

Vandiyadevan was stunned into silence.

The prince added, 'Warrior of the Vaanar clan, ask the Vaishnavite standing over there if you find yourself in doubt. Let's ask him what the prime minister has told him. Let's ask whether he didn't send a message saying the Buddhist monks would offer me the throne, and I must refuse in the presence of witnesses!'

This pronouncement stunned everyone else into silence too.

The prince then turned to the senapati and said, 'Aiya! Hear me out. It is true that the desire to win over the people of this land and rule as king is burning within me. It is my sister who has fanned these flames. She told me, "Thambi, you were born to be king. Your hands bear the sign of the conch and chakra. But there is no place for you here. So, you must head for Lanka and win the throne!" Ilaiya Piraatti would tell me this often, and I found myself taken with the idea. Therefore, I am, indeed, guilty. The emperor is justified in ordering that I be arrested and brought home.'

'Ilavarase, hold on for a moment. If such a desire has arisen within you, it can only be the good fortune of this land. The responsibility for such a desire awakening does not lie with you yourself, nor with your sister Ilaiya Piraatti. It is the emperor himself who is responsible. He has often told me of this wish for you himself and it was he who stoked the idea in your sister too. She merely conveyed your father's desire to you. And so, you're not guilty.'

'Senapati! If this is the case, what could stop me from going to my father? I will tell him what transpired as honestly as I can. Let these two men be my witnesses. And then, it is my duty to do as the emperor bids.'

Parthibendran now said in a fiery voice, 'Senapati! We've been wasting our time on talk. There is no point in hiding facts any longer. Let us tell the prince the truth. Will you, or shall I?'

'I will tell him myself. Hold on,' the senapati said. He looked about himself once, and then said, 'Ilavarase! I didn't want to sully your pure mind with this information, but ... well, we must tell you now about something quite disturbing. You are aware that Periya Pazhuvettaraiyar has married a woman called Nandini at his advanced age. She is no ordinary woman, but a witch if ever there was one! She has magical powers. She has used her maya-mantra to turn Periya Pazhuvettaraiyar into her slave. He rushes to fulfil her every wish. This great warrior from a clan of ancient standing ... look at what destiny has reduced him to!'

'Senapati, this is not news to me. The entire land has been speaking about the marriage and its effect on Periya Pazhuvettaraiyar for a while now.'

'Well, Nandini's magical powers have restricted their influence to her husband thus far. But ... and you must forgive me for saying these words, but ... now, it appears that ... that her influence extends to the emperor too. She has begun to weave her web around him. That is why such an order—an order to arrest you—was passed ...'

'Senapati! Be warned! I don't want to hear anything that might be an insult to the king. For as long as my father is alive, any order he passes—whatever the circumstances under which he issues such an order might be—is as scripture to me, and it will forever remain so!'

'We are not refuting that, ilavarase ... we are only afraid that it is not simply the emperor's freedom, but his very life, that is in danger. I did not know the whole truth about Nandini until yesterday. It was Parthibendran who told me. We must no longer hide this terrible secret from you.

'Do you remember the grand fight we had with Veerapandiyan three years ago, near Madurai? It was the final stage of the war. Your brother Aditya Karikalar, Parthibendrar and I consulted each other at every juncture of that battle. The Pandiya army was decimated. Veerapandiyan tried to escape just as he had before. Back then, he had made for the desert. Now, he hid in the forest. The three of us did not intend to let him get away this time round. We swore we would not return to Thanjavur without his head for a trophy. We chased after him ourselves. We finally learnt that he was hiding in a hut by a temple.

'Your brother had us remain outside to guard the place, and went into the hut. He came back with Veerapandiyan's head. We were triumphant, rejoicing in the fact that our goal had been attained. We didn't know of the drama that had played out inside that hut. The woman who had given Veerapandiyan shelter had stood between him and your brother, and begged Karikalar to spare her lover's life. Your brother kicked her aside and beheaded Veerapandiyan.

'Ilavarase! Do you know who the woman who tried to save the sworn enemy of the Chozha clan was? Nandini! She then married Pazhuvettaraiyar, who was well into his seventh decade, and became the Pazhuvoor Ilaiya Rani. Can you not see why she decided to do such a thing? It is simply to exact revenge for the death of Veerapandiyan! She intends to ruin the Chozha dynasty.

'No man who has ever met her could possibly have escaped her clutches … it is hard to resist her intoxicating beauty, the magical web she weaves. Vandiyadevan will assure you of this. And that Vaishnavite can tell you of a group that has taken an oath to rout the Chozha dynasty. It is Nandini who funds them when they need it. Ilavarase! Unfortunately, it appears the emperor has been caught in this witch's web. This is not the right time for you to speak of his word as scripture, and obey his orders.'

'Senapati! The things you have just told me come as a shock. However, this has only served to reassure me that my decision is right. When my father is surrounded by danger, is my place not by his side? Of what use is the Lankan kingdom to me? For that matter, of what use is my very life if I cannot carry out my filial duties? There is no point in talking about this any longer. No one must try to stop me now,' the prince said, firmly.

He then looked towards the pillar, behind which Poonguzhali was hiding, staring unblinking at him.

'Samudra Kumari! Come here,' he said.

Poonguzhali approached him.

'Penne! You have been of great help to me already. But I must ask another favour of you. Will you oblige?' he asked.

*Adada! What a question to put to this boatwoman! I came here in the hope of being of some little service to him. And here he is, asking me if I can do him a favour! It is as if I prayed to God to grant me a boon, and God responded by asking me for alms!*

Even as these thoughts flowed through Poonguzhali's head, she said aloud, 'Ilavarase! Your wish is my command. I await your orders.'

'Samudra Kumari! You said two huge ships filled with soldiers were waiting by the Thondaimanaru river for me. I must reach that spot right away. Will you show me to that place?'

'Penne! Refuse that request!' a stentorian voice said.

Poonguzhali was aware that it was the senapati's voice. She was being pulled out of her dream world and into a nasty conflict. She had been ordered to lead the prince into the very danger from which she had hurried to save him.

*Penne! Refuse that request!*

A thousand voices repeated those words, from every direction. The trees echoed the words, the pillars of the hall amplified them, and the birds sitting on the branches above screamed them out.

But then, an inner voice spoke louder than all of those. *Poonguzhali! Look at your luck! If you say yes, you will have two whole days with the prince. You can stay by his side for as long as it takes to guide him to that spot. You can drink in the beauty of his face unobserved when his eyes are turned elsewhere. The breeze that caresses you will caress him too. You can hear that beloved voice for two whole days. Adi penne! You dream of the impossible, for he can never be yours. But for two days, that dream will be your reality. Nothing will matter anymore after those two days! Poonguzhali, say yes!*

It was a gentle, coaxing voice that spoke next.

'Samudra Kumari! Why do you hesitate? Will you not do me this favour? Must I go all by myself, trying to find my own way?' the prince asked, and her heart beat so fast she could barely remain standing.

'Ilavarase! I will show you the way!' she cried.

The roar the senapati let out at this reached the bowels of the earth and radiated with such force that it all but sparked off an earthquake.

He then stepped forward and said, 'Ilavarase! I will not stand in the way of your wishes. But you must grant me this—it is my duty to protect you until you are in the custody of the men who are here to arrest you. Your friend spoke of multiple attempts to assassinate you last night. Those men have not yet been caught. We don't even know who they are. Forgive me for speaking my mind, but ... I cannot help suspecting this girl herself. How can we be sure she is not on their side? She could have made up this entire story about ships full of men waiting to take you into custody. When your friend Vandiyadevan grabbed her dagger and threw it into the bushes, we heard someone scream. Who was that person? We don't know any of these answers. I have no objection to this woman being your guide. Let her ride our elephant and show us the way. All I ask is that I accompany you until we spot the ships at the Thondaimanaru river. I will fall short of my duty unless I do this.'

The prince smiled at this little speech and said, 'As you wish. I will not stand in the way of your carrying out your duty.'

# 14

## 'THE ELEPHANT HAS GONE ROGUE!'

Once the decision had been made, the senapati called Parthibendran aside and had a short, private conversation with him. Then, he spoke to his soldiers and gave them a series of orders. It appeared he was dividing them into several groups, each assigned to a particular task.

Parthibendran took his leave of the prince, saying, 'Aiya, my mission has been unsuccessful. I leave alone, and without so much as a note from you. Karikalar will be furious with me. But what choice do I have? You insist on doing as you will, and I'll have to tell him there was nothing I could do to change your mind. Everyone present here is witness to my helplessness.'

'Must you leave in such a hurry?' the prince asked. 'Can't you spare the time to accompany the senapati and me to the Thondaimanaru river?'

'I will not be an accomplice to this charade. My ship is anchored at Tirikonamalai. I must return to Kanchi right away. I must tell Karikalar what transpired here as soon as I can,' Parthibendran said. He then turned to Vandiyadevan and asked, 'Are you not coming to Kanchi with me, Vallavaraya?'

Vandiyadevan took a while to recover from the sudden question, and then stammered, 'No. I wish to remain with the prince.'

'Wonderful. You're going to regret your decision,' Parthibendran said, as he left.

At the senapati's instance, several soldiers went with him.

Vandiyadevan turned to Azhvarkadiyaan and asked, 'What is the meaning of the Pallavan's words? He said I would regret my decision to not go with him? Do you understand what that might mean?'

'He and the senapati have put some secret plan in place. We'll figure out what it is soon enough. To be honest, it is this old man from Kodumbalur who is to blame for this whole sticky situation.'

'How is that? What could the senapati have done?'

'He's been scheming away. You're aware that a girl from his family has been growing up in Pazhaiyarai?'

'Yes, I know. You mean Vanathi Devi, don't you?'

'Yes. The senapati wants the prince to marry her, and for them to rule Lanka as king and queen. He's the one who instigated the Buddhist monks to make the offer they did. But did he have the discretion to do this quietly? No, spies have carried the news to Thanjavur. That was the reason for the prime minister's visit to Lanka. And that was why he sent me to seek out the prince. Vandiyadeva! Whatever happens, the two of us should guard our lives carefully. We're the only living witnesses to the prince's refusal of the throne, and we might be called upon to testify in Thanjai.'

The senapati had finished giving his orders. Except for a small group that stayed behind, his soldiers disappeared into the forest in various directions.

Finally, the prince's party was ready for departure. Arulmozhi Varmar, the senapati, Vandiyadevan, Azhvarkadiyaan and the four soldiers who had stayed on got up on the regal horses that stood waiting, while Poonguzhali mounted the elephant. The mahout climbed up after her.

For a while, they stayed on the Rajpath. But the going wasn't easy. There were too many people about. News of the prince's journey had spread. Back at the time, the northern part of Lanka had a large population of Tamils. They were keen to meet and cheer the prince, and the party had to pause as groups of people gathered and shouted, 'Ilavarasar Arulmozhi Varmar Vaazhga! Senapati Kodumbalur Velaar Vaazhga!' Sometimes, they went so far as to run after the horses. The men were barely able to move forward.

The prince consulted the senapati, and they decided to move off the Rajpath and travel through the jungle. It took some effort to get rid of the prince's aficionados and move into the trees. The forest presented another problem. It wasn't as easy for the animals to negotiate the uneven floor as it had been to walk on the road.

They hadn't gone far when a pond filled with lotuses appeared before them. On the opposite bank was another group of people waiting to welcome them. The moment they caught sight of the party, they began to cheer. The drums, cymbals and horns they had brought along with them, as if prepared for the occasion, started up.

'Hold on, let me see who these people are,' the senapati said, and went ahead to meet them. He returned soon enough, and announced, 'News of the prince's arrival has reached the villages nearby. They insist that they must welcome him properly.'

The villagers approached them.

They surrounded the prince, calling for his victory and well-being. But the cry that rose most often from them was, 'Eezhththarasar Arulmozhi Varmar Vaazhga! Long live the King of Lanka, Arulmozhi Varmar!'

The prince smiled. He gestured to a man who appeared to be the leader of the crowd.

'Why have they crowned me king of Lanka?' he asked, when the man stepped forward.

The man said deferentially, 'Arase! For a long time now, we have not had a real ruler. The land has suffered due to this. Everyone wants Ponniyin Selvar to be the king of Lanka. We beg that you accept. And when I say all of us, I mean Tamilians and Sinhalese,

Shaivites and Buddhists, monks and householders ... every single one of us, who have nothing else in common, has this one desire that binds us.'

The villagers had prepared a feast for the party. The prince could not refuse, and had to spend hours being welcomed.

As the prince was being felicitated, Vandiyadevan and Azhvarkadiyaan consulted each other.

'Thambi! Don't you see? Isn't it obvious these arrangements are all courtesy of the senapati? He's passed on the message that the prince will be going this way and prepared this grand welcome,' Azhvarkadiyaan said.

'Yes, it does seem to be the senapati's doing. But what is his motive? Does he think hearing the residents of the island voice their wish that the prince should rule will change Arulmozhi Varmar's mind?'

'Perhaps that too, but his main motive is to delay our journey,' Azhvarkadiyaan said.

'To what end?'

'I have no idea, but I've no doubt we're going to find out. Look at the prince's expression. Don't you see he isn't one bit happy with all this?'

Vandiyadevan looked at the prince. The face that usually remained unperturbed at the most testing of times was now flushed with fury. His eyebrows were knitted into a frown, and his eyes revealed that his thoughts were elsewhere.

Poonguzhali, in the meantime, was sitting by herself on the other bank of the lotus pond, lost in thought too. The journey had afforded her no pleasure. She had been looking forward to some time alone with the prince. She had hoped that he would speak to her, and that perhaps she might muster the courage to tell him something of her feelings. But it seemed there would be no opportunity for this. The prince was always surrounded by a crowd.

*All I'm going to get for my pains is the blame for delivering the prince to his enemies. Why should I wait for that? Why don't I simply run away from here, unnoticed by all these men? At least the senapati won't get angry and take me to task!*

*Chhe! What does it matter what the senapati does or feels? What does it matter what anyone does or feels? I'm not afraid of anyone's anger. But why must all my desires turn to dust? For how long will I stand, being slowly consumed by the fire that rages in my heart? Why am I even alive? Why doesn't a bolt of lightning strike me down? What's the point in wishing for it? I've wished for it so often, and nothing has happened. This life won't be taken from me unless I actively do something about it ...*

*Ah! What is this? Am I dreaming? No, no, this is not a dream! Why, the very knife that the prince's friend flung at someone in the ruin back there now lies on the ground. Someone has thrown it here. They must have intended to kill me. What a pity it missed its mark! Well, it's not all bad. At least I have the knife. The moment I have fulfilled my promise to him, the moment I have delivered him to his enemies, I will plunge this knife into my heart before his very eyes. Chhi, chhi! Why hurt him like that? No, I will watch him sail away, get on my own boat, row out to the middle of the sea and then kill myself. My beloved knife, you have come back to me. My gratitude to whoever flung you at me ...*

*Oh! But ... what if ... the target was not me, but the prince? Yes, the senapati himself warned that the prince would have to face great danger on his way ... if only it could be that someone would throw a dagger at him, and I could throw myself in the way and take it on my own chest? If only I could lie dying, dying for him, the blood pooling around me, and ...*

At this point, the grand scene Poonguzhali was creating took a life of its own, and seemed to play out before her eyes.

She had a knife in her heart, and blood was spurting out.

The prince came running up to her.

'Aiyo! You have sacrificed your life for me!' he cried.

As Poonguzhali's heart swelled upon hearing these words, the blood gushed out faster. The prince took her in his arms and held her to himself. The blood pouring out of her soaked his clothes and ran down his skin.

Poonguzhali laughed out loud and said, 'Ilavarase! Do you finally see, do you see what my heart has been carrying all this while?'

'Adi paavi!' the prince said, weeping. 'I knew that already. Is that why you sacrificed your life?'

Poonguzhali could not bear the joy of hearing these words. She laughed out loud, and ...

'Ei, you lunatic!'

Poonguzhali snapped out of her dreamworld and turned to the source of the voice. Vandiyadevan stood before her.

'The prince is already angry. The journey has been delayed enough. Don't add to his problems by tarrying now. Get up, it's time to go!'

Poonguzhali ran to the elephant, laughing. She hugged the knife to her chest and cooed at it as she mounted the elephant.

They had travelled a fair distance along the forest path when an incident occurred. From the thick foliage on the right side of the path came an arrow. There was no doubt the prince was the target. But Ponniyin Selvar was too quick for the weapon. He took hold of his horse's reins and turned the animal round in the nick of time, escaping the arrow by the skin of his teeth. It shot past his cheek and lodged itself into Azhvarkadiyaan's turban, carrying it away.

Azhvarkadiyaan touched his denuded head in surprise.

The senapati looked stunned, and everyone else stood frozen.

Poonguzhali wished the arrow had pierced her heart instead of Azhvarkadiyaan's turban.

Once he had found his tongue, the senapati said, 'Ilavarase! Do you see? What would have happened if you had set out alone, without us to escort you?'

He then ordered the soldiers to scour the forest and find the culprit. They returned empty-handed after a while.

The senapati settled down to plan the rest of the journey. He decided that they should move in formation, with the prince in the middle, and then began to design the formation.

'Senapati!' the prince called, 'I have a request.'

'A request? Command me!' the senapati said.

'I would like to reach Thanjai alive. I would like to prove to my father that I am innocent.'

'Your father would never doubt that, ilavarase!'

'Not just my father, but everyone must believe me. Once I've done that, I won't care for my life anymore. But I don't wish to die on my way to him.'

'Aiya! If there is so much as a hint of danger to your life, I will drive this Kodumbalur sword through my breast!'

'That will achieve nothing but inflict a terrible loss for Chozha Naadu.'

'What greater loss could Chozha Naadu suffer than that of its beloved prince? And if this Kodumbalur Velaar were to allow such a loss, how could he live with himself?'

'All the more reason for me to safeguard my life.'

'There is nothing more important in the world than that.'

'I have an idea.'

'Tell me, aiya!'

'For as long as I journey on a horse, I cannot avoid such risks.'

'You mean, something *could* happen to you?'

'Something *will* happen to me. But you know I have a way with elephants. They listen to what I say, and understand what I want them to do. You know of this skill of mine, yes?'

'Yes, aiya, and I'm aware you have travelled through most of this island in the guise of a mahout.'

'So, let me play mahout for now. Let the mahout take my place on the horse.'

The senapati was now in a dilemma. He looked about himself, hoping someone would be able to come up with a valid objection to the prince's idea. But everyone stayed mum.

'Aiya! But perhaps the mahout doesn't know how to ride a horse?'

'In that case, he can walk.'

'But that girl can barely look at you without running away to hide. What if she refuses to ride on the same elephant as you?'

'Well, in that case, she can walk too.'

'As you wish, ilavarase.'

The prince jumped off his horse and went up to the elephant. Poonguzhali's limpid eyes grew wide with surprise and large with eagerness. Arulmozhi bade the mahout step down and took his place. The interrupted journey resumed.

Poonguzhali was in the throes of ecstasy. She floated off the elephant's back and up into the skies, where she swam among the clouds. She had a sneak peek of Heaven, and understood what it was to feel joy that cannot be described. Was that the music of the gods she was hearing now? No, no, the gods couldn't make such divine music. It was the voice of the prince.

'Samudra Kumari! Does it cause you any chagrin to be alone on the elephant with me?'

'This honour is mine only because of the prayers and penance of seven births and rebirths, prabhu!'

'If this elephant were to go into musth and start running madly, would it frighten you?'

'For as long as you are by my side, even the sky splitting in two and falling on my head won't frighten me, aiya!'

'Where have you anchored your boat, Poonguzhali?'

'By the Yaanai Iravu Thurai, aiya.'

'On this bank or the opposite one?'

'On the opposite bank. I couldn't find a hidden spot on this side.'

'How did you cross the water, though?'

'When I came, it was low tide. So, I walked for the most bit, and swam the rest.'

'Would it scare you if the elephant got into the water?'

'It wouldn't scare me even if I were pushed into the water. I'm Samudra Kumari, aren't I? And wasn't it you who gave me that title?'

'Once we reach your boat, we'll climb inside. Are you sure you can row with both of us in it?'

'These arms have rowed the boat since I was ten years old. I don't have the hands of royal women, softer than the petals of flowers. Didn't your friend Vandiyadevar tell you I was the one who rowed him here?'

'He did. But today, we must go faster than you did that day. We must reach the Thondaimanaru as fast as possible.'

'Ilavarase! Why do you command me to do such a terrible thing? I rushed to the senapati to protect you from the very danger to which you now demand I deliver you. Why would you do that to a poor woman like me?'

'Poonguzhali, you're aware that my father—the emperor—is ill, aren't you?'

'I am, aiya! I'm also aware that the comet we've been spotting in the sky for some days now has people talking about ... about his ... about what it might portend.'

'You know, then, that he might breathe his last at any point?'

Poonguzhali was silent.

'If he were to leave this world, would it be right for him to go thinking that his son was conspiring against him?'

'The emperor would never believe such a thing of you. This is a conspiracy by the Pazhuvettaraiyar brothers!'

'I intend to prove my innocence to them, too.'

'Why, aiya?'

'Because I truly have no interest in ruling a kingdom.'

'What would you like to do, then?'

'I would like to get on a boat and travel the endless seas. I've heard that there are many, many lands across the oceans. I would like to visit all of them, and I would like to get to know the people on each land.'

'What a wonder this is!'

'What is?'

'The fact that you and I dream of doing the exact same thing. When you start this voyage, will you take me along?'

'First, I must do my duty. You *will* help me, won't you?'

'As you command.'

'Do you see the ropes on either side of your seat? Now, secure yourself to the seat using those.'

'Why, ilavarase?'

'Because the elephant is about to go rogue in a moment. Be careful and hold on, Poonguzhali!'

The prince then stroked the elephant and bent down to whisper into the animal's ear. The elephant's pace increased all of a sudden. The prince said something else, and that was it—the elephant broke into a run. Lifting his trunk, the animal let out a terrifying trumpet and then tore through the trees, uprooting trunks as if they were mere sticks. The world began to quake under his feet, and the birds took off in fright, their cries renting the air until the firmament echoed with screams of distress. The animals hiding among the trees came out into the open, running for their lives.

'Aiyayo! The elephant has gone rogue! What a terrible turn of events!' the senapati cried out.

In spite of the prince's warning, Poonguzhali felt her heart jump into her mouth. Her fear showed on her blanched face. She could feel the earth melt beneath her feet. She was plunging into a whirlpool, as was the prince, as was the elephant. She shut her eyes tight. The elephant was as a dark cloud rushing through the skies, driven by stormy winds, until he reached the shore.

This was the point known as Yaanai Iravu, the point where the southern and northern seas met. And it was at this point that the elephant delved into the water, and the resulting splash was as if the mountain Hanuman[1] was carrying had fallen into the sea.

15

# THE PRISON SHIP

All it took was a blink of the eye, and they had left Yaanai Iravu Thurai behind. Then, the trees of the forest flew backwards, as did the birds in the sky above. Boats, ponds, fields, villages, temples and mandapams danced into the recesses of the world they left behind as the elephant charged forward. For some time, a herd of deer kept up with the elephant, but then those fleet-footed animals fell behind too. The elephant alone went forward, forward, forward. How far and for how long, Poonguzhali couldn't say. She wondered if they were still in Eezham, or had left that island behind for another kingdom.

In this time, at his pace, the elephant could have circled Lanka thrice, couldn't he? No, no! The elephant was not going around the kingdom, but around the world. He was running from the southern pole to the northern pole. And she was doing a parikrama of the world, sitting on the elephant's back. Not just she alone, but the prince too!

When the elephant had first broken into a run as if in musth, Poonguzhali had known the taste of fear. Fear, mixed with the discombobulation of not knowing what was going on. The prince had turned back a few times and flashed her a smile. That had allayed her fears. Now, all she knew was boundless ecstasy. She didn't travel for long in this human world, on the back of an elephant in musth. She went right to the heavens. She was now seated on Airavata, the vaahan of Devendra.[1] Airavata was walking majestically through the celestial boulevards, while the trees on either side threw their softest blossoms at her. The Gandharvas flew by her side, drawing out the most beautiful notes from their instruments. The apsaras danced before Airavata. The stars shone on either side of the celestial boulevard as the devas gaped at the processions. Aeons passed.

Here, now, Airavata was slowing down. What, he had landed on the earth! He was walking through the forests of Lanka. The mahout stroked the elephant's forehead, and then whispered into the animal's ear. Chhe, chhe! He wasn't a mahout. He was Devendra. No, no ... he was the prince!

The elephant came to a halt before a pond that was surrounded by trees, and waited calmly.

Poonguzhali craned her neck anxiously, wondering whether there was a crowd waiting to welcome the prince on the other side of the pond. No, no one at all. She glanced back to see whether horses were following them. No, they weren't.

She looked at the pond. What was this? The blue and red water lilies came away in bunches and swam up to her. They then rose out of the water and surrounded her. They caressed her cheeks and shoulders, and every nook of her body. And then, the stalks of those cheeky flowers wound themselves around her and squeezed her so tight she could barely breathe. Poonguzhali had to shake them off, and it took such an effort that she felt she had been tossed around in a whirlpool by the time she finally rid herself of them.

The elephant gently lowered himself on to his forelegs, and then sat on his haunches. The prince slid off the animal's neck, and called, 'Poonguzhali! Have you no intention of getting off the elephant?'

Poonguzhali came to with a start.

'Aiya! It's hard to come back to earth from the heavens, no?' she mumbled, as she got down.

The elephant stood up, and made his way to a tree, from which he broke off a shoot and then began to chew on it.

Arulmozhi Varmar headed to the river bank and sat down. He signalled to a hesitant Poonguzhali to come join him.

When Poonguzhali did, she was startled by her own reflection in the clear water. The rapid journey and the joy she felt had daubed her cheeks red. Her complexion rivalled the red water lilies.

The prince said, looking at her reflection too, 'Samudra Kumari! I've grown very fond of you.'

The boughs of water lilies came back, and now kissed every inch of her body.

'Do you know why I like you so much?' the prince asked.

The sky and the earth and the pond and the lilies and the grass swam before Poonguzhali's eyes.

'Everyone I know desires that I act in accordance with his own will. But you, just you, agreed happily to do as I desired you to. I will never, ever forget this favour, Samudra Kumari!'

Poonguzhali's body turned into a yazh, the ancient Tamil instrument that resembles a harp. Her nerves were the strings of the yazh. Divine fingers strummed at her nerves and teased out music that could rival that of the Gandharvas.

'The senapati and Parthibendrar hatched a plot to prevent me from reaching the ship. The senapati sent men ahead to gather the villagers and prepare a feast for us every few kaadhams, in order to ensure that our journey was delayed. Parthibendrar has rushed to Tirikonamalai, and intends to reach the Thondaimanaru river before I do. And they thought they were so clever I couldn't see what they had planned. Thanks to you, I've outdone them, and escaped their schemes!'

All of a sudden, Poonguzhali realised just what she had done. In her delight that the prince had turned to her, she had undone every measure the others had taken to safeguard him. Now, she was in hell and Yama's goons were feeding her alive to the chekku.[2]

'Aiya! All of them were trying to save you from walking into the enemy's trap. I, on the other hand, am a sinner. I have escorted you to prison!' Poonguzhali said, and then broke into tears.

'Adede! What is this! I held you in such high regard. And now it turns out you're just like them!'

'I did not commit this crime of my own will. Your tender words turned my head upside down. I was intoxicated into insanity by what you said. Now, I have come to, and … I'm leaving.' With this, Poonguzhali jumped to her feet. The prince reached for her hand and held it gently, to stop her from leaving.

The apsaras from Devalokam were at a loose end, and saw this. They juiced the full moon and mixed its milk with sandalwood paste, which they then threw on Poonguzhali.

She lost every ounce of strength. She couldn't feel her legs. She sank back down, and started sobbing into her hands.

'Samudra Kumari! I wanted to tell you something important. But if you're going to howl like this, there is no point confiding in you. Let's just go.'

At this, Poonguzhali wiped away her tears and looked him in the eye.

'Now, that's better! You said a while ago that they were all trying to help me escape the enemy's trap, didn't you? Do you know why?'

'Out of love and affection for you. And I, alone, am a sinner, a schemer, a paadagi!'

'Hold on, hold on! Everyone has a whole lot of love and affection for me. But do you know why? Because some astrologers and palmists have told them that I will be the emperor one day. And so, each of them is competing with the other to seat me on the throne and dump a crown on my head. All from avarice!'

'Aiya! Why do you fault their desire to seat you on the throne? You are, after all, qualified not simply to rule *our* world but all three worlds!'

'Aha! You have jumped on this bandwagon too, have you? Penne! There is no prison quite like a palace, nor a sacrificial slab quite like the throne of an empire. There is no punishment worse than having to bear the weight of a crown on one's head. No one else will agree with my opinion. But I did think you would see the sense in what I say.'

Poonguzhali's eyelids fluttered like the wings of little butterflies. She looked at the prince with her large black eyes, so full of curiosity and eagerness and life and spirit.

'Samudra Kumari! Tell me the truth! If someone were to ask you to spend your entire life seated on a throne, would you consent to it?' the prince asked.

Poonguzhali thought for a while and then said firmly, 'No!'

'You see? Then why do you wish to foist such a punishment on me?'

'You were born into a royal dynasty, weren't you?'

'So what if I was? Thankfully, God doesn't wish to impose such a punishment on me. There are two contenders for the crown, my older brother and my great-uncle's son, who also wishes to be king ...'

'Oh, so news of that has reached your ears, has it?' Poonguzhali asked.

'Did you imagine that I wouldn't know? The throne in Thanjavur will not go unoccupied. And I have no desire to wear a crown and rule a kingdom!'

'What do you desire, then?' Poonguzhali asked.

'Now, that's a good question! One I'd like to answer too. You know how we went tearing through the forest on this elephant a while ago? I'd like to turn into a stormy wind and tear through forest and wilderness! I'd like to sail the seas and see the islands and the vast lands of which I have only heard tell! I'd like to climb the highest mountains and explore the wonders of each of these foreign kingdoms ...'

Poonguzhali listened with her mouth open, as if she ached to swallow each of the prince's words as they left his mouth. When she could no longer contain her enthusiasm, she interrupted him with, 'Aiya! When you go to all those places, will you take me with you?'

'These are only the dreams I nurse. Who knows whether they will come true?' the prince asked.

Poonguzhali left her dreamworld for the real one. 'Aiya! In that case, why must you go to Thanjavur now?'

'I was just coming to that. But you took me off on a tangent. Samudra Kumari! There is a mute woman on this island, a woman who cannot speak and who wanders about as if in a trance ... do you know her?' the prince asked.

Poonguzhali couldn't hide her surprise. 'I do know her. Why do you ask, ilavarase?' she asked, when she could finally bring herself to speak.

'I'll explain why later. But tell me, how do you know her? What do you know about her?'

'Aiya! I lost my mother as a child. It was that lady who showed me a mother's love. She is my mother, my guru, my god, my everything. What else do you wish to know about her?'

'Does she have a place to live? She seems to lead a nomadic life. Is there any place that she calls home?'

'On the way to Lanka from Kodikkarai, there is an island called Bhoota Theevu. There is a rock cave on that island. She can usually be found there. That was where I first saw you.'

'You saw me there, you say?'

'Yes. That lady has etched some beautiful illustrations on the walls of the cave. I first came across your face and figure in those pictures. When I saw you in the flesh in Kodikkarai, I was stunned.'

'Oh! Now, I see it all. The things that made no sense earlier now make sense. Samudra Kumari! Do you know of the relationship I share with that lady?'

'I figured there *was* some kind of relationship, but I don't know what it is.'

'Poonguzhali! The lady is my Periya Thayar[3], my elder mother. She ought rightly to have sat on the Thanjavur throne by my father's side.'

'What are you saying? Can this be true?'

'But destiny willed it otherwise. What can one do when the stars are aligned against one? It has struck me every so often that my father is being consumed by a hidden sorrow, some unspoken angst. It is only now that I have discovered the story behind his pain. My father believes that my Periya Thayar is dead. He believes, too, that her death was his fault. I must go tell him that she is alive. That will quell the ache in his heart, the suffering that is eating him alive. You know the emperor has been unwell, don't you? Our lives are so uncertain. All human life is ruled by uncertainty. One can never tell what will happen to whom at which time. For a while now, a comet has been spotted in the sky, the ominous Dhoomaketu. People have all sorts of theories about what it might portend. It's obvious that the emperor has been affected by this too. Under such circumstances, something terrible might happen to him. I must rush to his side before such an occurrence, and tell him what I've discovered. Samudra Kumari! That is why I'm in a hurry to get to Thanjavur. Do you now see how crucial your role in helping me out is?'

Poonguzhali, who had been listening intently to the prince's words, now let out a sigh. 'God! Why must you coat every one of the joys of human life with sorrow?' she mumbled to herself. Aloud, she said, 'Aiya! If I've been of any help to you, it is an honour that could only have been wrought by the good deeds I've done in a previous birth. But why did you need me? If only you had told the senapati and everyone else about this, wouldn't they have escorted you to Thanjai themselves?'

'I didn't want to share this with any of them. This wouldn't strike them as important, because all they want is to put me on the throne. And I didn't want to reveal my father's private matters to them. They wouldn't understand either. I have another favour to ask of you, Samudra Kumari! That is why I brought the elephant to a halt here. The same astrologers and palmists who have crowned me king have also predicted that I will face terrible dangers and trying times, dark periods during which I might succumb to some evil force. If something should happen on this journey I'm about to undertake ... if for some reason I'm not able to meet my father ... you must go to the emperor. You must find a way to meet him and tell him that my Periyamma is alive. If he wishes to meet her, you must take her to him. Will you do this for me, Poonguzhali?'

'There will be no terrible danger or trying times; no evil force will come anywhere near you. You will reach Thanjavur safely, scaring away those omens that dare close in on you!'

'Nevertheless, just in case something were to happen, you will do as I asked, won't you?'

'Most certainly, ilavarase!'

'Whom else could I entrust with such a crucial task? Tell me, if you can think of anyone.'

'Well, you have entrusted me with it. My obligations to you are now complete, are they not? Do I have your permission to take my leave?' Poonguzhali asked, her voice choked with tears.

'Aha! How can you leave? Who will take me to the Thondaimanaru river if you go? We haven't even seen the warships of Chozha Naadu. And you want to take your leave? Don't be angry now. You'll have to grit your teeth and bear my company for just a little while longer. Get back on the elephant and journey with me for a while. The moment we spot the tiger flag in the distance, you can part ways with me,' the prince said.

Poonguzhali didn't reply, but made her way towards the elephant. The prince followed. At his command, the elephant kneeled so that they could climb to their seats. Once they were seated, although the prince didn't ask, the elephant went fast.

'Samdura Kumari! I told you of my deepest desires, didn't I? Shouldn't you share yours with me? What do you like most in this world?'

'I like the rider of the buffalo, the lord of death, Yama. I like standing on the cliffs at midnight, watching the kolli vaai pisaasu. I lose track of time watching those flames.'

'What a strange woman you are!'

'What a *mad* woman I am, is what you mean. Just as your friend said. Don't worry, it won't hurt me. I like other things too. I like getting on little boats and rowing out to the middle of the sea. And when the storms catch me by surprise, I'm beside myself with excitement. Sometimes, the boat rides the crest of a monstrous wave and seems to go right up to the sky, right before sinking deep into the netherworld. There's nothing I like quite so much as that. When this elephant took off at a sudden run, as if in musth, I knew the same sort of delirious excitement!'

'Aha! Poonguzhali! If Lord Muruga had fallen for your lovely smile, he'd have been thoroughly snubbed. He was able to frighten Valli into marriage by getting his brother to play a wild elephant.[4] That plan would never have worked with you!' the prince said.

As they neared the Thondaimanaru river, Poonguzhali cried out suddenly, 'Ah! What's happened here?'

'What, what?' the prince asked.

'The warships carrying the tiger flag are not where I last saw them! What must you think of me now? I must seem exactly what the senapati believed I was, an accomplice of your enemies who has fooled you into coming here!'

'I would never think such a thing. Poonguzhali! There is absolutely no motive for you to con me into going anywhere with you ...'

'Why not, ilavarase? Love could be my motive, could it not? The entire world is agreed on the fact that you are the equal of Manmatha in good looks and Arjuna in valour and skill. A young girl overcome with desire for Ponniyin Selvar, who is Manmatha and Arjuna rolled in one, can come up with such a plan, couldn't she?'

'Penne! If the senapati were here, he might suspect such a thing. But there is no place in your heart or mine, nor in your head or mine, for such an insane notion.'

'Aiya! There is a princess in the Pazhaiyarai palace from that grand family of Kodumbalur, a princess called Vanathi Devi, isn't there? Would you speak of her in this manner?'

'Yes, yes, I haven't forgotten all that. The senapati and my sister have been scheming to dump that girl on me. And perhaps that young princess has bought into the fancy because she dreams of sitting on the Chozha throne someday. I'm not responsible for that, Poonguzhali. But why talk of all this? There is an important matter at hand now. Where did you last see the warships?'

'There, in that nook you see! I'm absolutely sure of it. I remember clearly,' Poonguzhali said.

'Well, perhaps they decided to move to a different spot, not too far away. Let's go up to the shore and check,' the prince said.

'If the ships have gone, it's a very good thing! Why must we go and search for them?' Poonguzhali asked.

'Aha! You might feel that way. But that would be the biggest betrayal of my hopes,' the prince said.

They walked up to the shore, and then along it.

As some readers might know, the Thondaimanaru river has an interesting history. About three hundred years before the events of our story, the Lankan prince Manavanna had surrendered at Kanchi, asking for shelter. The king of Mamallapuram had sent a grand army to help Manavanna win back his kingdom. The forces had landed at this very spot. Back then, the river had been a little stream. The bed had to be deepened and the banks widened so that the ships could anchor and the armies land. The stream had then been christened Thondaiman Aaru. The river had several bends at this point, and the foliage at the banks was thick. This allowed ships to remain hidden from the view of those approaching by sea.

It was in one of the deeper pockets of the Thondaiman Aaru that the ships sent to imprison the prince had been anchored earlier. They could not be spotted at that place now. That is to say, their masts and flags could not be spotted.

But when Poonguzhali and the prince got closer, a bizarre sight hit them. It appeared a ship had been dragged well on to the land, far from the water. Its masts and sails and flags were in tatters. No one seemed to be on board. Poonguzhali recognised this ship as one of the two she had spotted a couple of days earlier. The prison ship that had come to capture the prince was now imprisoned itself, stuck fast in the marsh. Poonguzhali found herself wonderstruck.

# 16

## BRIMMING WITH JOY

The prince whispered his magic words into the elephant's ear, and the animal lowered himself onto the ground. His two riders jumped off and hurried to the beached ship. The vessel looked pitiful. Its masts lay broken. They wondered whether someone might still be aboard the ship, or perhaps in the vicinity.

The prince clapped his hands to draw attention. Poonguzhali cupped her hands around her mouth and let out a birdcall. There was no response. They made their way to the side of the ship and climbed aboard. The floorboards on the deck were all broken. Water and sand had ruined the ship, and it was clear it was no longer serviceable. There would be no point in pushing it out back to the sea, even if they could. That was an impossible task. A single elephant would not suffice to pull the wreck on to the sea. They would need an army of elephants and men. Of course, the ship would have to be repaired first. That would take months.

The prince found the tiger flag among the shreds of the sails. He examined it. It was obvious that the sight distressed him greatly.

'Poonguzhali! Are you sure this is one of the ships you saw?' he asked.

'It appears so. Perhaps the other one has sunk entirely into the sea and is lost forever?' Poonguzhali asked. Her tone was cheerful.

'Why so much joy at that?' the prince asked.

'Why wouldn't the fact that the ships that came to capture you sank before they could complete their mission fill me with joy?' Poonguzhali said.

'Your joy is misplaced, Samudra Kumari. Something terrible must have happened. It hurts me that a ship bearing our emblem has suffered such a fate. I can't imagine what misfortune might have befallen it. Where are the soldiers and traders that the ship must have carried? What has become of them? I'm all confused. You think the other ship must have sunk?'

'I think it might have. Which would be a very good thing.'

'Not at all. That cannot be. Perhaps the captain of the other ship saw this one get stuck in shallow waters and steered his own further out to sea. I don't see why this one came so close to the shore in the first place. The traders of Chozha Naadu have been sailing for thousands of years. They could not have made such an amateur mistake. Even so, the occupants of the ship must have escaped. And then boarded the other ship. Come, let's go look for it!'

'Where will we look, ilavarase? The sun has set, and dusk has fallen. We won't be able to see a thing,' Poonguzhali said.

'Samudra Kumari! Where did you leave your boat?'

'My boat is a long way back. The reason we arrived as fast as we did was that we took the land route, and that too with you riding the elephant as hard as you did. If we had come by boat, we wouldn't have reached before midnight,' Poonguzhali said.

'All right, come, let's go search by the shore before we lose all light,' the prince said. 'The trees here are blocking my view of the sea. Perhaps the other ship is anchored some distance out.'

They left the elephant to graze, and went towards the sea. The waters were calm, strangely so. They couldn't spot the merest hint of a wave. As far as the eye could see, the ocean was as a pale green mirror. It met the blue sky far, far away.

There was no ship, or even a raft, out on the sea. A couple of birds flew towards the shore, but there was no other sign of life. The prince took it all in for a while, and then said, 'Right, let's go back to the shipwreck.'

The two of them began to trace back their path.

'Poonguzhali, I'll never forget this favour you have done me. But the time has come for us to part,' the prince said.

Poonguzhali was silent.

'Didn't you hear me? I've decided to stay by the wreck. The senapati and his entourage are bound to arrive here at some point. Once they reach, I'll consult them, weigh our options and then make a decision on what to do next. But there is nothing for you to do here any longer. Why don't you head back to your boat and leave? Remember what I told you about my father ...'

Poonguzhali hesitated. She then leaned against a tree trunk and held one of its branches, as if for support.

'What is it, Samudra Kumari? What happened?'

'Nothing, ilavarase! I will take your leave here. Please take care of yourself.'

'Are you angry, Poonguzhali?'

'Angry? What right does someone like me have to get angry with you? I know my place. I won't overstep my bounds.'

'Why did you suddenly pause then?'

'It isn't anger but exhaustion, ilavarase. I haven't slept a wink in two days. I think I'll rest for a while here, and then go look for my boat once I wake up.'

It was the day after the full moon night. The sun had set, and the moon was rising. Its delicate rays now fell on Poonguzhali's face.

The prince examined her moonlit face. He noticed how gaunt and tired she looked. It is natural for a lotus in full bloom to close its petals at moonrise. But the petals on this lotus-faced beauty hadn't simply closed. They had worn and faded to the point of withering.

'Penne! You said it has been two days since you've slept. How long since you've eaten?'

'More than two days, but for as long as you were by my side, I knew no hunger.'

'What a callous fool I have been! The rest of us have been feasting away every few hours, and I didn't so much as ask you whether you've eaten! Poonguzhali, come with me! Let's go to the shipwreck. I remember seeing a few sacks of grain there that had spilt their contents. There must be more provisions aboard. Let us make dinner, eat and then go our separate ways.'

'Aiya, I know I'll fall asleep the moment I eat. I can feel my eyelids drooping even now.'

'So what? Eat and sleep all you like. The elephant and I will keep watch. Once the sun has risen, you can go back to your boat.'

With this, the prince took Poonguzhali's hand and led her back to the ship. He noticed that her legs were shivering. Not in all the seven worlds above or below would he find another girl who cared so much for him, he thought, and the realisation brought tears to his eyes.

When they reached the ship, they sensed smoke coming from behind it. Perhaps its occupants had returned from somewhere? If they saw two intruders, things might go awry. So, Poonguzhali and the prince slowed their pace, careful not to make a noise. But they couldn't make out any speech even when they were almost upon the ship. There was no clue as to how many people were there, or who they might be.

But the smell of sweet potatoes being cooked wafted towards them. The prince's priority was to feed his starved companion. And so, he asked her to stay where she was, and hurried around the ship. He could see the silhouette of a woman. She was cooking a meal. It didn't take him long to recognise her. It was Kaveri Amman, the mute woman who had been looking out for him all this while. He ushered Poonguzhali forward. His saviour didn't seem surprised by their arrival. She greeted them without a word, and bade them eat. The meal she had prepared tasted more delicious than any royal feast the prince had ever had.

Once they had eaten, the three of them made their way onto the deck of the ship. The moon had risen high. They could see the point at which the Thondaimanaru river met the sea, and the placid waters beyond. The green of the dusk had morphed into gold, as the rays of the moon stroked the waters.

In spite of the vast open space and the surrounding waters, the air was so humid that they found themselves sweating through the night. There was no breeze. The prince remarked about this to Poonguzhali, and the elderly woman must have deciphered his words, for she pointed towards the moon. It had an ash-coloured halo around its circumference.

'They say that a circle of ash around the moon is a sign that there will be a storm right after,' Poonguzhali explained. 'It indicates winds and rain.'

'Well, let the storm take its time, but I wouldn't mind a strong wind right now!' the prince said.

He then turned to Poonguzhali and asked how the lady could have arrived so quickly.

'Oh, that's hardly a challenge for my athai[1]. She's worked a lot of wonders bigger than this,' Poonguzhali said. 'Besides, her love for you is boundless. And love gives one the strength to do just about anything, doesn't it?'

The woman understood this exchange too, and responded by turning Poonguzhali's face gently towards something. When Poonguzhali looked, she first saw the elephant they had ridden. Not far away was a thoroughbred horse, standing regally on the sand. It was a startling sight.

'She rode that horse here? She knows how to ride?' the prince asked in surprise.

'There is nothing Athai doesn't know. She rides horses and elephants. She knows how to ply boats. And sometimes, I think she simply rides the wind. She goes from one place to another in no time, and none of us can figure out how.'

The prince was now preoccupied with something else. He had taken a closer look at the horse, and could tell its origins.

*How did an Arabian stallion arrive here? And how did this lady get her hands on the stallion?* he wondered to himself.

Poonguzhali said something to Oomai Rani through a series of gestures. Yes, reader, we're going to call her 'Oomai Rani' from here on out.

She then interpreted her aunt's response to the prince's question. Apparently, the horse had glided out of the water onto the shore. Oomai Rani had stroked him and her affection had tamed him, allowing her to ride him.

The prince could barely contain his surprise. Even so, he noticed that Poonguzhali's eyelids were drooping.

'You said a while ago that you were sleepy. Let me not keep you up any longer. Go, lie down!' he said.

Poonguzhali seemed to have been aching to hear these words. She wasted no time in finding a spot to sleep. She pulled a tattered piece of sail around herself, and within moments, a slight change in her pattern of breathing indicated that she was asleep. But even in her sleep, her lips moved gently, and her lovely voice whispered:

*Alaikadalum oyindirukka*
*Agakkadaldaan ponguvaden*

*When the sea drifts to sleep,*
*Why do waves crash within?*

Aha! Why, this was the very refrain Vandiyadevan had been singing under his breath all through the time they had spent together! He must have picked it up from her. When Poonguzhali was awake, he must ask her to sing him the whole song, the prince thought.

His thoughts then turned to the Oomai Rani. Aha! Waves *did* crash within everyone's heart. It was natural for the mind to be in turmoil every now and again, for the heart to weep with agony. But what could equal the sorrow of this woman, who didn't even have a voice to give expression to her inner unrest? How much misfortune, what joys and sorrows, frustrations and fears and hurt and rage were contained within that heart? And for how long she had held them all within herself!

Oomai Rani now came up to the prince and sat by him. She stroked his hair gently, and then touched his cheeks as if they were the delicate petals of a blossoming bud.

The prince did not know how to react at first.

Then, he bent down to touch the elderly woman's feet and then brush his hands against his eyes.[2] She took his hands in hers and touched them to her own face. Soon, the prince's fingers were wet with her tears.

Oomai Rani then signalled to him to go to sleep. He need not worry, she wanted to say, she would stand guard.

The prince didn't think he would sleep a wink that night. But he made a show of settling in for the night so she wouldn't worry. For a long time, his heart remained in turmoil. Then, the slightest breeze relieved the heaviness of the air. As his body cooled down, his mind found some rest too. Perhaps there was a chance he would sleep, he thought.

But when the prince eventually dozed off, he was troubled by the most bizarre dreams. He flew through the skies on an Arabian stallion. He passed through several celestial worlds until he reached Devalokam itself and found Indra waiting with his elephant Airavata. Indra asked him to climb onto Airavata, and then led him to his palace, where he invited him to sit on his gem-studded throne.

'Oh, I have no desire for the throne. I would like my Periya Thayar, the Oomai Rani, to sit here,' the prince said.

Indra laughed and said, 'Let her come here first, and then we'll see.'

He then offered the prince nectar.

Arulmozhi drank it and then said, 'Oh, this isn't as tasty as the waters of the Kaveri river.'

Indra then led the prince to the antapuram, where all the celestial maidens and matrons lived.

Indrani looked at the prince and said, 'Whichever of these maidens you find most beautiful, you can marry.'

The prince scanned the celestial beauties and said, 'I'm afraid not one of them is the equal of Poonguzhali in beauty.'

At this, Indrani turned into Ilaiya Piraatti and asked, 'Arulmozhi! Have you forgotten Vanathi?'

'Akka! Akka!' the prince pleaded. 'For how much longer are you going to enslave me like this? The prison of your love is even crueler than the Pazhuvettaraiyar brothers' dungeon! Please, release me! Set me free! Or, just keep me bound to the palace as King Virata did with his son Uttara Kumar.[3] Let me while away my days in song and dance!'[4]

At this, Kundavai put a delicate finger to her coral lips and said, her eyes wide with surprise, 'Arulmozhi! Why have you changed so much? Who has turned your head like this? Yes, it is true that love is a form of enslavement. I'm afraid you'll have to be bound by it.'

'No, Akka, no! You're wrong. There is such a thing as love that doesn't enslave, love that sets one free. Do you want me to show you? Here, let me call her. Poonguzhali! Poonguzhali! Come here!' he called.

Let us leave the prince to his dreams for now, and roll back in time for a bit to see what has been happening with the subject of those dreams, Poonguzhali. There she is now, waking up to the sound of hooves just as dawn is breaking.

Poonguzhali got up and saw Oomai Rani climb onto the horse. She ran to stop her from leaving, but the horse had disappeared before she even reached the shore.

The sunrise was beautiful. Her heart was full. She felt an excitement she had never known before. She looked up at the deck of the ship. The prince was asleep. Poonguzhali walked along the riverbank, listening to the melodious birdsong.

She spotted an enormous parrot on a branch of one of the trees by the shore. The bird did not seem perturbed by her presence. Instead, the parrot turned to Poonguzhali as if asking her what she was doing there.

'Kili Thozhi![5] The prince will leave shortly. Then, you'll be all the company I have. You'll talk to me awhile, won't you?' Poonguzhali asked.

Just then, she heard a voice call, 'Poonguzhali! Poonguzhali!'

At first, she thought it was the parrot. But, no. The voice was coming from the ship. The prince was calling for her! She took off at a run. But when she reached the deck, she saw that the prince was still asleep. She went closer, and saw his lips part as he mumbled, 'Poonguzhali!'

Every core of her being trembled with delight. She bent down and touched his forehead to wake him.

The prince opened his eyes, his sleep and dream interrupted. He saw that the sun had risen. Poonguzhali's face bloomed before him, like a lotus at dawn.

'Why did you call out my name?' she asked.

'I? I called out your name? I must have been muttering in my sleep. You sang in your sleep last night, didn't you? Am I not allowed to speak in mine?' the prince said, smiling.

He then jumped up. 'How late it is! Where is Periamma?'

He looked about himself.

Samudra Kumari told him that Oomai Rani had left on a horse early in the morning.

'A good thing! Samudra Kumari, you seem to have rested well. You may leave too. I'll wait for my friends here. I'm going to explore the ship,' the prince said.

Poonguzhali suddenly cried, 'There, over there!'

The prince looked in the direction she indicated. Far away on the ocean, he could discern an enormous warship. A boat from the ship was nearing the shore. It had five, perhaps six, occupants.

'Aha, we'll get to know everything now,' the prince said.

Afraid that the boat would sail away without spotting him, he jumped off the deck and ran down to the shore. Poonguzhali ran after him. The elephant, too, followed them at his own unhurried pace.

When they reached the shore, they saw that the warship was moving further away from them, while the boat was approaching. Poonguzhali, who had been lurking in the background, now stepped forward, eager to see who was aboard.

Her enthusiasm lifted the prince's spirits. Through all his worries, he found himself smiling.

There were plenty of reasons for him to worry. He couldn't shake off the feeling that he should have been on the ship that was sailing away, leaving him behind. And that was not all. He had the feeling that someone who should have been on the approaching boat was missing. Yes, there they were, the senapati, Tirumalai, the four soldiers and the boatmen … but where was the young man of the Vaanar clan? Where was Vallavarayan Vandiyadevan? The valorous young man with his ebullient spirit, his intrepid heart, his independent soul, the messenger whom Kundavai trusted so much, was nowhere to be seen. They had only met two days ago, but the prince felt he had known Vandiyadevan all his life. When he didn't see him on the boat, the prince had the sinking feeling that he had lost a rare gem too soon.

The boat had not quite reached the shore when its occupants jumped off. The senapati ran towards the prince and pulled him into a tight embrace.

'Aiya! What a thing to do! How could you give us such a scare? We were beside ourselves with worry! How did the elephant's musth abate? How calmly the rogue elephant stands now! Ilavarase! When did you reach this spot? Did you see the Pazhuvettaraiyar brothers' ships? Where are they?' he asked, all in one breath.

'Senapati! I'll fill you in on my story later. Tell me first, where is Vandiyadevar?' the prince asked.

'That impulsive boy is on that ship,' the senapati said, pointing towards the vessel that was speeding away.

'What! Why? Whose ship is that? And why is Vandiyadevar on board?' the prince asked.

'Aiya! I'm barely able to think. My mind is all muddled. Please ask this Vaishnavite here. He knows more about that young man and his impulses than any of us does,' the senapati said.

The prince turned to Azhvarkadiyaan and said, 'Tirumalai! Why is Vandiyadevar on that ship. If you know, tell me, quickly!'

# 17

## EERIE LAUGHTER

At this juncture, we're obliged to tell our readers what transpired once Poonguzhali and the prince took off on the elephant, leaving the rest of their crew behind. Let us travel back in time once more!

'The elephant is in musth!' the senapati cried.

Upon hearing this, everyone took off in chase, without pausing to think whether this might really be the case. Naturally, it was impossible for their horses to catch up with the prince's elephant. Once they reached Yaanai Iravu Thurai, their journey was impeded further by an incident. As usual, Vandiyadevan had pushed ahead of everyone else on his mission. His horse jumped into the water in pursuit of the elephant, and was promptly caught in the marsh. It took an enormous effort to free the horse. However, the poor animal was deemed unfit for the impending journey.

Senapati Boothi Vikrama Kesari now had no clue what he was supposed to do. He could not stop banging his head with his large hands.

'I've never in my life made a more foolish mistake!' he lamented. 'All of you are simply standing there and staring at me! Think, my men, think! What do we do now? How do we save the prince? If something, anything, occurs to anyone, tell me!'

At this point, Azhvarkadiyaan stepped forward and said, 'Senapati, something just occurred to me. May I speak?'

'Are you waiting for an auspicious time? Tell me, fast!' the senapati snapped.

'The prince's elephant cannot really have been in musth.'

'What are you on about? Then, who's in musth? You?'

'No one is in musth. The prince must have suspected that you were delaying the trip on purpose. He wanted to leave us behind and surge ahead. He's commanded the elephant to do just that. We all know that the prince has a way with elephants.'

The senapati realised Azhvarkadiyaan was right, and at that thought he felt at peace.

'All right. But even if that is the case, we must go to the Thondaiman Aaru—to find out what happened, if nothing else.'

'We must. Our only option is to go to the shore and see if we can find a boat that will ply us there.

Or, we must wait for Parthibendra Pallavar to arrive with his ship.'

'Vaishnavare! You're a sly one. You must have told the prince what you suspected.'

'Senapati! I haven't spoken to the prince since we embarked on this journey.'

The party then went eastwards, along the seashore.

Our readers might be familiar with the northern part of Lanka. During the era in which our story is set, the northern region was known as Nagadvipam— 'snake island'. The ocean made inroads from both sides, separating this portion from the rest of the country. The tiny strip of land that connected the two parts was known as 'Yaanai Iravu Thurai'. At times, when the tide was low, one could cross easily on foot from one side to the other. At other times, one could not make the crossing without a boat. Herds of elephant would get into the water and cross to the northern part, thereby giving the isthmus its name, 'Yaanai Iravu'. It is said that in ancient times, elephants were captured and exported on ships from this place too.

On the day the entourage went looking for a boat, most of the vessels had gone to Mathottam or Tirikonamalai. They were already aware of this, but the senapati and his men were still hopeful that there might be a stray boat or two that would take them across. They kept a constant lookout, and finally saw a tiny vessel rowed by a fisherman. Although he had no one else to help row the boat, the fisherman agreed to take them across the sea once he knew it was the senapati of Chozha Naadu who was asking.

It wasn't hard to get to the other side, but they were still some distance away from the point where the Thondaimanaru river joined the sea. One option was to go through the forest, but with its thick foliage and wild undergrowth, it wouldn't offer an easy journey. The other option was to use the same boat to row along the shore until they reached the sangamam. They settled on the latter.

The fisherman rowed on until midnight, at which point he said he was too tired to go any further. The others offered to help, but he said that that would not serve the purpose. The journey ahead required expert manoeuvring, for they would have to change direction often. There were stones and tricky bends that could destroy the boat. The fisherman insisted they would have to wait until morning.

The senapati and his men were tired too. And so, they went ashore and found a grove of trees under which they could shelter.

Vandiyadevan was not happy about any of this. He quarrelled with Azhvarkadiyaan.

'This is all because of you!' he said.

'What is because of me?'

'You're never entirely honest. I've been noticing this since I first met you in Kodumbalur. You make a grand show of speaking openly. But you always keep half the secret to yourself. You knew exactly what the prince's intentions were the moment he mounted the elephant, no? Why didn't you tell me? Then I'd have climbed up alongside him. The prince whom we found with such difficulty is now lost again. How am I going to go back to Pazhaiyarai and explain this to Ilaiya Piraatti?'

'Your duty ended when you delivered the scroll. What explanation are you obliged to offer?'

'That is not the case. My duty will not end until I escort the prince safely to Kundavai Devi. And it seems you're happy to be an obstacle.'

'No, appa, no! I'm not going to be an obstacle. I'm going to take my leave of the senapati tomorrow and go my way.'

'Of course, you've done what you came to do. You've delivered the prince to his captors. I've had my suspicions about you right from the start. Now, you've confirmed that I was right.'

They bickered for a while but were too sleepy to continue after a point, and eventually collapsed like they had been knocked unconscious.

It was Azhvarkadiyaan who woke first, having felt the first rays of the morning sun on his face and heard the sounds of oars hitting water. He sat up and looked about himself. What he saw made him start. Some distance away, on the water, was a large warship. A boat was heading towards it from the shore. There were three men aboard, apart from the boatman.

Azhvarkadiyaan didn't take long to discern that it was the same boat that had brought them here the previous day.

He also figured out from where the warship had emerged. Not far from the spot where they had rested for the night, the river bed was deep, the waters having burrowed into the earth over time. A thicket of trees must have hidden the anchored ship at night. Once dawn had broken, the ship had set sail.

But whose ship was it? What was its origin? And destination? And why was the boat heading towards it? Who were the occupants of each vessel? The questions flashed at lightning pace in Azhvarkadiyaan's mind, even as he called out to the senapati.

The entire group woke up to his panicked cries.

First, they saw the ship, and the senapati said, 'Ah, that's a Chozha Naadu ship all right. It must be the one the Pazhuvettaraiyar brothers have sent. Perhaps the prince is on board? Aiyo! We slept late. What a mistake it was!' He then asked, 'Where is our boat? We can still catch up!'

He then spotted the boat out at sea and said, 'Adade! That is our boat, isn't it? Who is on board! Dei, adei, you, the boatman! Stop! Stop!'

The boatman might have heard him, or not. But he did not stop the boat. He kept rowing towards the ship.

Vandiyadevan, who was watching all this, only heard one sentence. 'The prince is on board.'

There was no place in his mind for any other thought. And he had no doubt as to what he should do next. His legs knew even before his brain did, and they ran towards the sea. Vandiyadevan pushed at the waters and ran towards the ship. Thankfully, the waters were shallow and he was able to go some distance before he felt his feet give way. The bed dropped all of a sudden and he lost his footing.

'Aiyo!' he cried. 'I am dying! I will sink! Help! Help! Someone save me!'

He could hear laughter from the boat. And then voices. The boat stopped and then started gliding towards him. The boatman reached out and pulled him on board. Wet and shivering, Vandiyadevan looked at his fellow travellers.

One was clearly not from Tamizhagam. He appeared to be an Arab. How had he got here, Vandiyadevan wondered, and then turned to the others. They had covered part of their faces, but it was clear they were Tamil. And they looked familiar too. Where had he seen them before? Ah, they were the men whom he had seen with Parthibendra Pallavan the other day. Azhvarkadiyaan had said these were the men who had tried to assassinate the prince. Oho ... and he had seen one of these men earlier himself. Wasn't that man the mantravadi, Ravidasan? He had mimicked an owl's cry when he had come to the Pazhuvoor Ilaiya Rani's palace! Right, there was only one explanation—they knew that the prince was aboard the ship, and were headed towards it. Aha! What a good thing that he had had the instinct to run into the water. The prince would have been in terrible danger! Now, he would not have to fight alone.

The boat was making for the ship. The passengers were silent. Vandiyadevan couldn't bear this silence. He decided to make conversation.

'Where are you headed?' he asked.

'Can't you tell? We're headed for that ship,' the mantravadi said.

His voice, muffled by the cloth he had pulled over part of his face, had an eerie tone.

'And where is the ship headed?' Vandiyadevan asked.

'One has to wait until one reaches the ship to find out,' Ravidasan said.

No one spoke after this. Only the omkara of the water around them could be heard.

Now, it was the mantravadi who broke the silence.

'And where are you headed, appa?' he asked.

'I'm headed for the ship too,' Vandiyadevan said.

'And then, where?'

'One has to wait until one reaches the ship to find out,' Vandiyadevan echoed.

The boat had neared the ship by this time.

A rope ladder dropped down from the deck. The men climbed up, one by one. Vandiyadevan held on to its rungs and strained his ears. He could hear the sound of speech from the deck. A foreign language. He hurried up, and jumped on to the deck.

'Where is the prince?' he cried, as he looked about himself.

The sight that met his eyes shook his courage.

Standing before him were Arab men with a terrifying aspect. Each could pass for a demon. They stared at him intently. No one answered his question.

Vandiyadevan had the sense that he had made an awful mistake. This was not a ship from Chozha Naadu. It could not be. The men on board were not Tamil traders. They were Arab traders, who had probably brought their grand stallions to sell.

The prince could not possibly be on board. Vandiyadevan had rushed into a trap. How was he to escape? He peeped overboard, and saw the boat sailing away.

'Oi, boatman! Stop!' he cried, and went to jump into the sea.

But before he could act on this impulse, a hand stronger than the vajrayudha wielded by Indra wound itself around his throat. A pull, a shove, and Vandiyadevan found himself lying on his back in the middle of the ship's deck, dazed.

Blinded by rage, he rose and rammed his fist into the jaw of the man who had grabbed him. That six-footer fell back against another man, and both went down from the force of Vandiyadevan's blow.

Hearing a low growl behind his back, Vandiyadevan turned—just in time to knock off a dagger that would have plunged into his back if he hadn't swung around.

The hilt bounced off his hand, onto the edge of the bow of the ship, and then disappeared into the water.

The next moment, Vandiyadevan found himself surrounded. His captors spoke in a language he did not understand. Their leader issued a series of commands in an authoritative tone. Some of the men disappeared, only to return with iron chains with which they bound Vandiyadevan's hands and feet. They shackled his arms to his body, and then four men carried him down into the ship's hold. They threw him onto a stack of wood, and then bound him to a log before they left.

The ship was heaving mightily. As it rocked, the wooden rods fell all over him. He was helpless to move them away, bound as his limbs were.

*If I manage to escape this time, I swear I will never act on an impulse again. I will do as Azhvarkadiyaan does, think a thousand times before I choose my course of action,* Vandiyadevan thought to himself.

That was when he heard it. Eerie laughter, close at hand.

It took a huge effort for Vandiyadevan to turn his face and see who had joined him in the hold. It was Ravidasan. The cloth with which he had masked his face was gone.

'Appane, I came to hunt the tiger of the Chozha clan. The tiger hasn't been captured, but the fox from the Vaanar clan has, it seems. So our hunt was not in vain!' Ravidasan said.

Remember, readers, the prince's party had only seen Vandiyadevan get on the boat. They did not know what had happened after. The boatman too was oblivious to what had happened on the ship. He rowed back to land, only for the senapati and the rest of the men to climb onto his vessel. They knew there was no point in trying to catch up with the ship now. They had decided to make for the point where the Thondaimanaru river joined the sea. The other ship could be there. The prince might be on board *that* ship. Whether he was or not, they would at least learn what had happened.

They interrogated the boatman, but he didn't know much.

'I was fast asleep,' he said. 'Someone woke me up at dawn, and promised me a lot of money if I'd row them out to the ship. I figured I'd be back before you all woke up. That's all I know.'

This is what transpired in the prince's absence.

Now, Azhvarkadiyaan recounted everything *he* knew to Arulmozhi Varmar.

'Ilavarase!' he said. 'When Vandiyadevan ran out to the sea and plunged into the water, for a moment I wanted to follow him. But I've always been wary of the sea. I'm not a good swimmer. And I had my doubts about the ship we saw. I didn't think it was likely you'd be on board. I wasn't even sure it was a Chozha Naadu ship. I told the senapati of my doubts, and we decided it was best to come here and then take stock. It's only after seeing you well that our minds are at rest,' he said.

The prince, who had been listening to every word, replied, 'But *my* mind is not at rest, Tirumalai! Vandiyadevan is on that ship. The Pazhuvettaraiyar brothers will throw him into the dungeon!'

At this, the senapati said, 'Ilavarase! Why must we put up with those two overstepping their bounds? Just say the word, and I'll end their reign before the next full moon day! I'll throw them into their own dungeon!'

'Aiya! Please do not even dream that I will commit the slightest act that runs contrary to my father's will and wish,' the prince said.

Just then, they heard the sound of a horse's hooves, running at a great pace towards them. They turned as one, and saw the horse come to a stop. They stared in wonder at the rider. The horse did not wear a saddle or a bridle. And the rider, who had been guiding the majestic stallion without reins, was a woman.

## 18

# THE DEATH OF THE KALAPATI

The prince knew right away who the woman on the horse was. He hurried to the animal, and Poonguzhali ran alongside him. The others followed more warily.

Oomai Rani had dismounted by the time the prince and Poonguzhali reached her. She glanced at the entourage behind them anxiously, and then made a series of gestures to Poonguzhali.

'Periamma says she has seen something strange in the forest. She wants us to go there with her,' Poonguzhali interpreted.

The prince decided to go right away. He asked Poonguzhali to check with Oomai Rani whether the entourage could come along. Oomai Rani thought for a while, and then nodded her consent.

On the way, the men couldn't stop talking about the horse on which she had arrived. An Arab stallion, a thoroughbred, the kind deployed in war ... how could she have got hold of such an animal? No army had landed on these shores recently. There had been no war in the vicinity. And yet, she had a warhorse of the highest pedigree. How had that come about?

We've already seen the shipwreck by the Thondaimanaru river. From that point, the shore curved in the south-eastern direction for some distance. The water had carved out lagoons of various dimensions over time. It was from one such lagoon that the other ship, spotted by Vandiyadevan and the others that morning, had emerged.

Now, Oomai Rani led them along the shore, towards the south-east. She went into the dense forest. The prince's interest was piqued. Something of great significance must have occurred, or she wouldn't take him along this path, he thought.

And, all of a sudden, the mystery was solved right before their eyes.

They came to a clearing, beyond which they could see the backwaters. Corpses lay scattered by the shore. The stench of decomposing bodies mingled with the smell of dried blood. The men in the prince's entourage had seen many wars, and were no strangers to such odours. But a sense of foreboding and dread filled their hearts. They knew instinctively that what had occurred here was something particularly terrible.

When they went closer to the bodies, they realised the men who had been killed were all sailors from Tamizhagam.

'Quick, quick, look and see if anyone is still alive!' the prince cried.

His men ran to each of the prone bodies, checking for life.

Oomai Rani took the prince's hand and led him towards a tree, some distance away from the bodies. Lying against the trunk was a horrible figure. It was a man all right, but one could barely believe it was human. Not an inch of his body had been spared. There were gory wounds on every limb. A gash on his head leaked blood over his face. This was a man praying for death to relieve him of his misery. Every prolonged second was, clearly, torment.

Yet, when this man saw the prince, his livid, swollen face brightened for a moment. He opened his mouth, as if he wished to speak. But his mouth only spouted more blood, and further distorted his appearance.

The prince ran to his side.

'Water, quick!' he cried out.

The man said, 'No, ilavarase, I don't need water. This lady brought me water some time ago. If she hadn't come when she had, I would be dead by now. Aiya! I have paid the price for the treachery I have committed against you. My karma has caught up with me, and I will be spared punishment in the afterworld.'

The prince squinted at the man's face, and then said, 'Ah! Kalapati!' (You see, back in the day, just as the head of the army was known as 'senapati', the captain of a ship was known as 'kalapati'.) 'What are you saying, kalapati? What happened here? You speak of treachery against me? I would never believe you could betray me! I don't believe it!'

'Aiya! It is your purity of heart and goodness of nature that lead you to speak as you do. I came to arrest you at the command of the Pazhuvettaraiyar brothers. Here is the order,' the kalapati said. He reached for a scroll lying on his lap with shaky hands, and then held it out.

The prince glanced at it and then said, 'How is this evidence of your betrayal? You have come to fulfil the emperor's orders. And once I heard of this order, I came in search of your ship myself, to make your work easier. How has such a disaster occurred in the meantime? Tell me, quickly!'

'I will have to tell you quickly, or I will never get to tell you at all,' the kalapati sighed. He then told the story that follows, with great difficulty, taking several pauses for breath. It was with a desperate effort that his body stayed alive until he was finished.

The kalapati had started off from Nagapattinam, commanding two ships and armed with the emperor's order. His heart was not in this mission. But he had been in no position to flout the emperor's orders. The Pazhuvettaraiyar brothers had issued a series of strict instructions to him. Once he reached the Lankan shore, he was to anchor his ships at a discreet spot and find out where the prince was. He was then to set out to meet the prince personally, and hand over the scroll signed by the emperor. Under no circumstances was Senapati Kodumbalur Velaar Boothi Vikrama Kesari to get wind of the order before the prince saw it. Once the prince had read the scroll, he was to be given a choice—he could accompany the kalapati of his own volition, or he could refuse, in which case he was to be arrested and hauled to the ship. The Pazhuvettaraiyar brothers had also sent some of their trusted men along with the kalapati.

The kalapati had left on his mission, his heart weighed down by a great burden. Most of his men had had no clue why they were sailing to Lanka. This had only heightened his sorrow and guilt. He had wondered how he would break it to them. Once they had anchored the ships, he had gone with some of his men to Kangesan Thurai to inquire into the whereabouts of the prince. They had learnt that Ponniyin Selvan was travelling deep in the southern part of the island.

By the time the group had returned to the ship, all the sailors who had accompanied them knew why they were here. Remember, some of the Pazhuvettaraiyar brothers' men were among them? They had spread the word. The sailors had surrounded the kalapati the moment they saw him, and started firing questions at him.

'Are we truly here to arrest Ponniyin Selvar?'

'Have we been ordered to capture the prince?'

'Is it true that Arulmozhi Varmar is to be imprisoned?'

The kalapati had told them the truth, and then added, 'We serve the crown. We are bound by duty to obey the emperor's command.'

'We will not do this!'

'We cannot do as you ask!'

'This is not the emperor's command, it is that of the Pazhuvettaraiyar brothers!'

'What do you intend to do then?' the kalapati had asked.

'We are going to head for Mathottam, and join the prince's forces.'

'The prince is not in Mathottam!'

'In that case, we will surrender to Senapati Kodumbalur Velaar!'

The kalapati had not been able to convince the men. Only ten men or so who were loyal to the Pazhuvettaraiyar brothers were willing to obey his orders. What could ten men do to subdue two hundred?

'Fine, then go right away. Get lost, do what you will and pay the price for it! I'm going to do my best to carry out my duty,' the kalapati had said.

The majority of the sailors had been keen to board one of the ships and make for Mathottam. But some had objected to this, saying it would be a better idea to go by land. They had convinced the others, and so they had all disembarked from one of the ships. In their hurry, they had forgotten to secure the anchor, and so the ship had drifted towards the land and fallen to its sorry state.

The kalapati had not wished to remain on board the other ship with his small band of men. At Kangesan Thurai, he had heard that a ship full of Arab traders had arrived at Mullaitivu some days ago, and that it had met a sorry end. The survivors of that shipwreck were lurking about the shore of the Thondaimanaru river. And so, he had steered the one remaining ship in his command further down the shore, and anchored it safely. He had then led his men ashore, and consulted them on the course of action they should take next.

Eventually, they had decided that the kalapati would go alone to seek out the prince, while the rest of the crew guarded the ship. This had been the kalapati's idea. His men had told him they were worried for his safety.

Before he could as much as respond, they had heard blood-curdling screams that made their hair stand on end. In an instant, they had been surrounded by the Arab sailors. It had been an unexpected ambush; the kalapati and his men had not even carried their weapons to the shore. They had given it their all, but it was not an even battle, and the Arabs had triumphed.

'Ilavarase! I knew my wounds were fatal, but I crawled to this point, wanting to stay alive until I had told someone what had transpired here. Ilavarase! I have had the honour of meeting you in person, and telling you this myself. I have paid the price for my treachery. Please forgive me!' the kalapati said.

'Kalapati, you have only done your duty. I have nothing to forgive. If there is such a thing as a Veera Swargam, a Heaven for Battle Heroes, you will reach that paradise. I have no doubt of this,' the prince said, stroking the kalapati's burning forehead.

The other man's tears cleared away the blood on his face.

It took him an enormous effort to hold the prince's hands in his, and touch them to his eyes in a gesture of devotion. As the prince's hands grew wet with the kalapati's tears, Ponniyin Selvan welled up too.

It was not long before the kalapati's life seeped out of his body.

19

# HUNT FOR THE SHIP

The men accompanying the prince gathered the corpses of the fallen—the kalapati and his sailors—and then laid them out on dry wood to cremate them.

As the flames rose into the air, Senapati Boothi Vikrama Kesari noticed that tears were streaming down the prince's face.

'Aiya! Are you crying because these traitors are dead? They have only got their just deserts for setting out to arrest you. Why should that sadden you?'

'Senapati! They are not traitors. And it is not their deaths that saddens me. It is the fact that Chozha Naadu is going through such a terrible period.'

'The terrible period was wrought by the Pazhuvettaraiyars. It has lasted as long as they have. It is not new, is it?'

'It is new, indeed. Whoever heard of mutiny? When sailors refuse to obey their captain, the kingdom is truly in a dire state. Senapati, this is but a small indication … I worry that such instances of insubordination may erupt across the empire. This great kingdom that was established by Vijayalaya Chozhar will be run to the ground. Must I be the cause of its downfall? You know, in the Mahabharata, they say wolves and jackals howled when Duryodhana was born. They must have howled when I was born too!' the prince said.

'Aiya! The moment of your birth was heralded by a series of auspicious signs! Every good omen one could think of … why, every astrologer who sees your horoscope …'

'Enough, senapati, enough! My ears have soured from hearing this over and over again. Let my horoscope be what it is. What matters is the present moment. It is now time for us to part. Senapati, I ask this of you—if the men who refused to follow the kalapati's orders are to approach you, please do not welcome them into your ranks. Have them arrested and sent to Thanjavur.'

'Ilavarase! We have heard only one side of the story. We don't know how the sailors felt or what they thought or why they acted as they did. How can you make a decision based on the kalapati's testimony alone? Is that just or right? Come with me. When the sailors approach us, please hear them out and then make a decision …'

'Aiya, that is not possible. Do as you wish. I cannot delay a moment longer. I must leave right away. Where is the boatman?' the prince asked.

'Where must you be, ilavarase? Why do you ask for the boatman?'

'Need you ask? I must make for the ship that Vandiyadevan has boarded. It was for love of me that that brave soul hurried towards the ship on which he thought I was, and he has now put himself in terrible danger. How can I leave him to the tender mercies of those Arabian pirates? Have I not sinned enough already? Must I add *snehadroham*[1] to the list?'

'Aiya! You haven't committed a single sin to my knowledge. Even if you claim you have, no one in the world would agree. Vandiyadevan is a hothead. He does not think before he acts. How could you possibly be responsible for the consequences of his very nature? Where does friendship figure in this equation? Ilavarase! I don't like your calling a stranger, who came out of nowhere, your "friend". It is only people of equal stature and status who can be friends, surely?'

'Senapati, I do not wish to waste time on idle talk. Whether he is my friend or not, there exists such a thing as gratitude in my dictionary. Every great scholar and poet, starting with Tiruvalluvar, has spoken of the importance of gratitude. There is an adage that goes, "A member of the Chozha dynasty never forgets a good turn." I don't want to disprove it. I'm going to leave right this moment, and find that ship!'

'How will you go, and where will you search, ilavarase?'

'I will go on the boat you brought.'

'You're trying to hunt a tiger with a rabbit for your ride! How can you possibly hope to catch up with that enormous ship that is equipped to sail the deep seas with this little boat? And even if you do catch up, what do you intend to do?'

'I'll sail on the boat. And if it were to splinter, I'll swim over holding on to one of its broken pieces. The ship that has captured Vandiyadevan could sail across the seven seas, and I will not give up my chase. I will save my friend, or die trying. Now, where is the boatman?' the prince said, even as he scanned their surroundings for the boatman. He noticed Poonguzhali talking to the man. The mute woman was with them too. The prince hurried towards the group.

When he got closer, he saw that there were tears in Poonguzhali's eyes, and she was fuming at the boatman.

'Aha! What happened now?' the prince asked.

The boatman threw himself at the prince's feet. 'Ilavarase! I have sinned! I have made a terrible mistake, all for the love of money. Please forgive me!' he cried.

'What is this now? Poonguzhali, are all of you out to drive me insane? Won't you tell me what the matter is?'

'Ilavarase, I have hidden something from you, for shame. This man is my older brother. It was he who ferried across the two men who are trying to kill you. He brought them here from Kodikkarai, and has been hanging about here at their instance. And this morning, it was he who rowed them to the ship. Your friend got on the same boat ...' said Poonguzhali.

'Prabhu! Kill me. Cut off my head! I did not know they were such terrible men. If only I had known, I would not have brought them across the ocean. Please, kill me with your own hands!' the boatman said.

'Appane! Your life is priceless to me at this moment. Come, let's go. Row me to the ship! Think of it as penance for your sins. Come on, let's leave!' the prince said.

The boatman dragged the boat from the sand, out into the water. The prince squinted at the ocean.

'There! I can still see the ship! We can catch up!' he said.

The senapati, too, looked at the ship in the distance.

'Ilavarase! How fortuitous! It is like fruit accidentally falling into milk to sweeten it!' he said.

'What, you of all people have something positive to say, senapati?'

'The ship we see is not the one you think it is. It isn't the one on which Vandiyadevan left, but the one that Parthibendran commands. It is arriving from Tirikonamalai. And it is headed for us. Can't you see?' replied the senapati.

'Yes, yes, all the better. Parthibendrar's intentions may be completely different, but he is here at just the right time. We can now hunt the tiger with a lion for our ride! But I can't wait for the ship to arrive. I'll meet it with the boat ...'

'Ilavarase! Please permit us to accompany you on the ...'

'Aiya, the greatest favour you can do me is to stay back here along with everyone else. Tirumalai, this goes for you as well. You're not a fan of the ocean, if I remember right?'

'Yes, aiya. My intention was entirely to stay back. My orders are to look after you for as long as you are on the island. The prime minister is in Madurai. I must go to him and fill him in on what has been happening.'

'Well, you may do so. Poonguzhali, you must stay back. Don't worry about your brother. I will look after him. You said you'd left your boat somewhere around here, didn't you? Please go your way. I will never forget the help you've given me. Tchah, tchah, what is this? Stop crying! Wipe your tears. What will people think?'

With this, the prince went to Oomai Rani and bent to touch her feet. She stopped him, and kissed his forehead instead. Once he had received her blessings, the prince leapt into the boat. His entourage stood on the shore, staring at the boat as it sped away. The prince stared back at them. And his eyes rested on Poonguzhali, whose own eyes were blurred by tears. Wonder of wonders, he thought ... as one went further away, figures ought to get smaller. And those of the men on the shore did. But Poonguzhali's face alone got bigger, and bigger, and bigger. It came closer and closer to the prince even as his boat went further out.

The prince's skin broke into gooseflesh. He averted his eyes. He remembered the incident from his dream the night before And, over the din of the waves, he heard Ilaiya Piraatti's voice say, as clear as ever, 'Thambi! Don't forget that Vanathi is here, waiting for you!'

# 20

## THE ABATHTHUDAVIGAL

One cannot put into words Parthibendran's shock on seeing the prince make his way towards his ship. Imagine that the god one has been praying to by undertaking years of severe austerities and penances, appeared before one, and then said, 'Ask of me any boon!' That's how Parthibendran felt. But what was Ponniyin Selvan doing, alone on a boat? What had become of the Pazhuvettaraiyar brothers' ships? Perhaps the prince had mistaken Parthibendran's ship for one of the prison ships?

It was evident soon enough, though, that the prince was under no such illusion. The moment Arulmozhi climbed aboard the ship, he briefed Parthibendran on everything that had happened since they'd last met, without waiting to be asked.

'Vandiyadevan is now on the ship the Arabs have seized. We must save him somehow,' he said.

Parthibendran was beside himself with joy upon learning the fate of the Pazhuvettaraiyar brothers' ships. 'Everything has gone as it should. If only that hot-headed boy hadn't gone and done such a moronic thing! But, whatever he's done, we can't leave him to the tender mercies of those foreigners. That ship can't have gone far. We'll be able to catch up,' he said, and then sent for his own kalapati.

'Oh, there's no cause for worry!' the captain said. 'If the wind keeps up, we'll be able to catch up with that ship by sundown. Where's it going to go, anyway? It will have to head for Kodikkarai and then stay by the shore.'

However, Lord Vayu's intentions were not quite in line with their interests. The God of Wind decided to slow down. As the day wore on, the breeze dulled. By afternoon, it had come to a complete stop. The sea was as glass, without so much as a wave in it. Lord Surya glared down at the sea, sending balls of fire into the water, and the humidity made everyone feel clammy. When they looked at the ocean, they got the sense that they were inside a boiling vat of oil, waiting to be fried. When the sun's rays caught a ripple, it looked like the sea of fire from hell.

Even with all the sails up, the ship would not move. As the sea came to a standstill, the flapping of the sails died down too. The canvas did not so much as brush against the masts. The absence of even that susurrous sound filled the men with unspeakable sorrow. The prince became frantic with worry for his friend.

'How terrible for the wind to stop like this! How long will this last? When will the breeze blow again? Will the other ship make a getaway?' he asked.

Parthibendran turned to the captain again.

'The standstill won't last long,' the kalapati said. 'This means a storm is brewing somewhere. There's a fair chance it will hit us. Or, it could change course and spare us. But whether or not we are caught in the storm itself, the sea will turn turbulent soon enough. It seems impossible now, when we cannot see so much as a ripple in the ocean, but by tonight, we'll be sailing on the crest of waves as high as mountains and riding troughs deeper than the netherworld itself.'

'But if the storm hits us, we're in danger, aren't we?'

'No ordinary danger. We'll simply have to pray for the gods to save us.'

'So, it will be near impossible for us to catch the ship.'

'Ilavarase! The seas and storms know no favourites. That ship is in the same situation as ours. It will remain as still as we are at this moment.'

'Perhaps they're sailing by the shore?' the prince said.

'In that case, those aboard have a chance to escape. But the ship's fate is sealed,' the kalapati said.

'However grave the danger is, as long as one's near and dear ones are by one's side, there is no cause for concern,' the prince said. As he spoke the words, Vandiyadevan's cheerful face and Poonguzhali's adoring eyes danced before him. Where could they be now? What could they be doing? What could they be thinking?

Well, readers, we must now head back to Vandiyadevan, whom we have left in great danger. It isn't good form to abandon him. He was in the ship's hold, with bundles of goods, wooden rods and sundry discarded items for company. He had been bound to a rod. He had just come out of a near trance. Why had he got himself into such a predicament? Why could he never pause to think before acting? Whose ship was this? Where was it headed? How had these Arabs and Ravidasan got into cahoots? What did they intend to do with him? He couldn't make sense of anything. His dreams of a bright future would remain dreams, it appeared. But he had escaped from graver dangers than this, hadn't he? This would not finish him off. He would make his way out of this trap too! A sense of doom alternated with this sense of inspiration. Well, there was no reason to lose hope for as long as there was life in his body and he was able to think straight. He would wait and watch.

With this thought, he took in his surroundings. It was pitch dark, and he struggled to discern even the outlines of objects at first. As his eyes gradually adapted to the dimness, he realised that there were several weapons heaped together, not far from where he was. His body had been bound tight, but they had been careless with his arms. He wiggled one hand free, and then tested its reach. Ah, he could just about reach a cutlass. Well, that would allow him to cut off the ropes that bound his torso and legs. And then, what? He had been locked inside the hold. How was he to get out? And even if he did, would he be able to take on an entire crew of Arabs, along with Ravidasan and his friend? And even if he did manage to kill them all, what was he to do after? He was no sailor. He had no clue how to navigate the ship through the ocean.

No, no, there was no point in jumping into a new mess. He must wait—just for once, *wait* and watch. There must be some reason for the men having kept him captive rather than put him to death right away. What were their plans? He wouldn't know unless he waited. Yes, waited.

But as time passed, Vandiyadevan found his patience put severely to the test. The hold was becoming increasingly hot. He had an image of being roasted slowly in an oven. Sweat poured down his back. He had never imagined that a sea voyage would entail such discomfort. He couldn't help contrasting this journey with the one he'd undertaken on Poonguzhali's boat. The cool breeze had caressed his body then ... but now he was in a furnace.

Suddenly, he sensed a slight change. Something was different. Yes ... the ship had stopped moving. It seemed to have come to an absolute standstill. The humidity increased even further. He was dying of thirst. His throat felt dry. No, he could not hold out. He would have to reach for the cutlass, free himself from the ropes and search the ship for water. A vessel this big had to have stores of water!

Vandiyadevan scanned his surroundings again. There was a pile of coconuts in one corner. Aha! Which fool wails for ghee when he has butter? The coconuts would quench his thirst and slake his appetite. Vandiyadevan freed both his hands and was just reaching for the cutlass when he heard footsteps. Someone opened the door. He drew his hand back.

Ravidasan and his friend entered the hold. They stationed themselves on either side of Vandiyadevan.

'How do you find the journey, appa? I trust you're comfortable?' Ravidasan asked.

Vandiyadevan gasped, 'The thirst ... it's killing me! Some water ... please, some water!'

'Ah, we're thirsty ourselves. But those fools did not stock the ship with water!' Ravidasan said.

'Kali is thirstier than any of us. She's bloodthirsty!' the other man said.

Vandiyadevan turned to the man and squinted at his face. Why did he look so familiar?

'Don't you recognise me, thambi? Have you forgotten? The Kuravai Koothu at the Kadambur palace was followed by the Devaraalan getting into a frenzy, remember? He went into a trance and said, "Kali is asking for a sacrifice! She's asking for the blood of a thousand-year-old line!" Don't you remember?'

'Ah, now I do! You're the Devaraalan!' Vandiyadevan muttered.

'Indeed I am. We came to Lanka, so we could quench Kali's thirst with the sacrifice she seeks—a prince from an ancient bloodline. We didn't succeed. We tried to send that Veera Vaishnavite to Vaikuntha, but that didn't work either. But here you are, uninvited but most welcome! I suppose Kali will have to resign herself to the blood of an inferior line!' the man said.

'So why delay it?' Vandiyadevan asked.

'Why would we slaughter a brave young man such as you without all the ceremonial rites in the middle of the sea? We must take you ashore, parade you through the town, call all the priests and lay you down on the sacrificial slab before we chop off your head, no? Most importantly, the high priestess must be there.'

'Who is the high priestess?'

'Don't you know? The Pazhuvoor Ilaiya Rani, who else?'

Vandiyadevan thought for a while, and then said, 'Well, if those are your intentions, give me some water. Or I'll die of thirst right here.'

'We told you, thambi, there is no water.'

'I thought you were a mantravadi?'

'Well said. I've chanted the mantras. The wind has died down now. But there will be whirlwinds by night. A storm will strike and the skies will open. Rain will pour down upon us.'

'Of what use is rain to me? You're on deck, but I'm here. I can't so much as taste the rain.'

'You're welcome upstairs. You'll be free to stick out your tongue and swallow all the rainwater you can. If you do as we say.'

'And what do you say?'

'We say those Arab monsters should be gifted to Samudra Raja.'

'Why?'

'They want to sail the ship to Kalinga. We want to head for either Kodikkarai or Nagapattinam.'

'But there are six of them, and they seem savage.'

'Three of the six are asleep. The other three can barely keep their eyes open. If the three of us kill the sleeping ones, we'll be evenly matched.'

Vandiyadevan was silent.

'What do you say, thambi? If you agree to go along with our plan, we'll free you right away.'

The prince's disapproving face appeared before Vandiyadevan. No, he would never agree to this. The prince would never forgive him for killing an opponent in his sleep.

'I cannot. It is despicable to kill a man in his sleep.'

'You fool! These Arabs assaulted the sailors from Chozha Naadu when they were all asleep, don't you know?'

'Why must I sink as low as they did?'

'Well, it's your call,' Ravidasan said.

He then went up to the heap of weapons and chose a sword. The Devaraalan went for a staff with an iron tip. The men left the hold, but did not lock the door. The moment he heard them go upstairs, Vandiyadevan reached for the cutlass and freed himself. He then cut open a coconut and drank its tender juice. He ate the meat of the coconut and then drew a sack over the others in the pile.

He made his way to the weapons and chose a large blade, one that was fit for use in war. He took his stance, ready to run up at any moment. He heard two dull thuds and then a couple of splashes. Two bodies had been thrown overboard. There were screams and cries, sounds of flesh hitting bone and metal clashing against metal, all from the upper deck.

Vandiyadevan rushed out. He saw that the four remaining Arabs had surrounded Ravidasan and the Devaraalan. He let out a battle cry and ran towards the Arabs. One of them turned, spotted Vandiyadevan and ran towards him, sword in hand. Vandiyadevan knocked his opponent's sword into the sea. The Arab then folded his hand into a fist and aimed for Vandiyadevan's chest. Vandiyadevan stepped aside neatly, and the Arab fell into the space he had emptied.

The force with which he hit the deck made him reel, and as he got up he was knocked out by a crossbar of the mast.

A second Arab sailor clashed with Vandiyadevan and, after a brief duel, was thrown overboard.

The 'mantravadi' and the Devaraalan were not war veterans. They could barely take on an Arab opponent each. It wasn't long before they tired. But the commotion Vandiyadevan had created and the fact that their friends had not returned to fight by their side distracted the two remaining Arab sailors and they turned as one. Ravidasan and the Devaraalan seized the opportunity to stab them when they weren't looking.

Once it was all over, the three victors panted, trying to catch their breath.

'Appane, you came at just the right time! How did you get out?' Ravidasan asked.

'Must be one of your mantras at work. The ropes that bound me fell off by themselves, and this sword flew into my hand,' Vandiyadevan said.

'And what about your thirst?'

'A coconut appeared out of nowhere and hovered over my head. Then, it broke itself and fed me some of its juice.'

'Oho! You're something!' the Devaraalan said, as he and Ravidasan burst into laughter.

'Thambi, we were putting you to the test. We kept your ropes loose and left weapons at your disposal.

We even made sure the coconuts were kept where you could see them,' Ravidasan said.

Vandiyadevan couldn't gauge whether they were telling the truth. He didn't respond.

'Appane! Think before you answer. Do you want to live? Do you want to get back ashore safely, and meet your friends and family? Do you want rewards and remuneration, stature and social standing, titles and treasure? Tell us if you wish for these, and join us ... you can have it all!' Ravidasan said.

'Didn't you kill men who were asleep?' Vandiyadevan asked.

'Only two of them. The third woke up before we got to him. If you'd only joined us a tad earlier, our task would have been simpler.'

'How is it right to kill men in their sleep? How were you able to bring yourselves to do that?'

'He's afraid of a mustard seed, and wants to take on giant pumpkins!' Ravidasan scoffed. 'Look, if you want to join us ... '

'You go on about joining you ... who are "you"?'

Ravidasan turned to the Devaraalan. 'There's no point in hiding anything from him now, is there? He will either join us, or get swallowed by the sea. Let's tell him the truth, no?' he said.

'Tell him, tell him everything!' the Devaraalan sang.

'Look, thambi. We're the Abaththudavigal[1] of Veerapandiyar. We've sworn to protect him with our very lives ...'

'… and failed. Aditya Karikalar was the victor!'

'And how did he gain that victory? Because of the foolishness of a silly girl! She overestimated her powers of seduction. She thought she could charm the King Cobra of the Chozha clan, and make him dance to the tunes of her pungi.[2] The cobra did dance. But it shot out poison too. Our king's head rolled onto the dust. And they carried that head all the way to Thanjavur and paraded it too. Aha, Thanjavur, Thanjavur! Just you wait and watch what becomes of that city, thambi!'

As he spoke these words, Ravidasan's bloodshot eyes seemed to spit fire. His body trembled. His two rows of teeth grated against each other, making a horrifying noise. The Devaraalan, too, displayed a similar mien.

'Well, what's happened has happened. What do you intend to do about that? You can't bring the dead Pandiyan back to life, can you?'

'We can't bring Veerpandiyar back to life. My mantras are not powerful enough. But we can destroy the man who killed him, and the men who stand by that murderer. We will decimate the Chozha snakes, every little infant of that dynasty. Will you join us? Tell us now!'

'And once you're done with this destruction and decimation? What next?'

'We will crown whoever our maharani chooses as our next king.'

'Who is this maharani?'

'Don't you know, thambi? The woman who is acting as the Pazhuvoor Ilaiya Rani now!'

'In that case, the promise made to Madurantakar ...'

'He is one of the snakes, too, isn't he? A baby snake?'

'And Pazhuvettaraiyar?'

'Ah! You think we're going to make him our king? Ha! It is to use his money and influence that ...'

'Your maharani has chosen to make her home with him.'

'What a genius you've proven to be, thambi!'

'And the silly girl whom you blame for the death of Veerapandiyan?'

'The very same Pazhuvoor Rani. She promised she would heal our king, when he fell in battle. She has failed to fulfil that promise. We thought she had proven herself a traitor, and were all set to burn her alive. But she swore an oath along with us that she would avenge herself against his killers. So we've spared her. And she has been doing as she promised. Without her help, we could never have come this far.'

'But you haven't achieved anything yet, have you?'

'Have some patience, appane! Wait and watch,' Ravidasan said.

'He's wheedled everything out of us. But he hasn't responded properly to a single question we've asked,' the Devaraalan said.

'Thambi, what is your decision? Will you join us? Who knows, your fortune might hold out. You might

be crowned the king of southern Tamizhagam for all
we know! What do you say?'

If he had been in the same situation at an earlier
time, Vandiyadevan would have agreed to switch sides.
But he had spent three days in the company of the
prince, and that had changed his perspective. His
opinion of plotting and scheming and cheating had
altered. What used to strike him as strategic now
seemed revolting.

And so, he changed the subject. 'Tell me, first …
how did you capture this ship? How did you befriend
the Arabs you just sent to meet their maker?' he asked.

'By the power of my mantras, appane! We bought
horses from these very men at Tirikonamalai. And we
tried to chase you all with those very horses. We saw
the prince get off at Yaanai Iravu Thurai. We were
determined to precede him here, and used a shortcut.
When we arrived, we saw that our old friends had
seized the Pazhuvettaraiyar ship. Apparently, they had
been shipwrecked near Mullaittheevu. They asked us
if we would be their guides, on the new ship. It's not
often that such a stroke of luck comes your way, now!'

'And what stroke is that?'

'We heard the junior cobra talk to his senapati.
We understood that he intended to return to Chozha
Naadu one way or another. You see, thambi, there's
a mute ghost in Lanka. This ghost has in her powers
mantras that can counter mine, and has been saving

the prince all this while. But she cannot follow us to Chozha Naadu.'

Vandiyadevan thought back to the events of their first night in Anuradhapuram.

Ravidasan suddenly burst into laughter.

'To what do you owe this joy? What makes you laugh now?' Vandiyadevan asked.

'Oh, nothing, I simply thought of the nature of these Arabs, and it made me laugh. They strike us as savage creatures, no? They'll behead a man with all the fuss of skinning a banana. But when it comes to horses ... oh, the care they take! They told us they only ride the horses once they've fitted them with iron shoes. We're savages, they said, for making them run barefoot. It is a sin to sell us horses, they said. Do you know what happened this morning?'

'Do enlighten me.'

'We all boarded the ship. Once the sails were unfurled, the ship sailed off. When we were already some distance from the shore, we heard hooves. They swore it was one of their horses, and you wouldn't believe the fuss they made. They insisted that a search party set out and bring the horse back. One of their men set off to look, and they had us go along with him.'

'And then?'

'And then we couldn't trace the horse. We didn't manage to capture that animal, but we did capture you. What a piece of luck that these men are so obsessed with their horses!'

'All this is well and good, but this boy is yet to answer our question,' the Devaraalan said grimly.

'I'll answer, aiya! I'll answer right away. I've sworn allegiance to the Chozha dynasty, and I will never go back on my word. I will never join you.'

'Have you joined the Velakkaara Army? Have you sworn their oath?'

'Nothing of the sort.'

'Then why do you hesitate? You're a warrior. You should choose the side that promises all the right opportunities, shouldn't you?'

Vandiyadevan did not tell them that it was not just his word that held him back. He did not tell them of the sidelong glances that Ilaiya Piraatti had graced him with, of those beautiful eyes for which he could lay down his life. And then there was the unparalleled friendship he had struck with the prince. Once one had become his friend, could one ever switch allegiances?

'You can say anything you want, but there is nothing in the world that could persuade me to throw my lot in with your murderous mob,' Vandiyadevan said.

'Well, then, you might as well prepare to sacrifice your life to Samudra Raja,' Ravidasan said.

21

## WHIRLWINDS

There was no movement at all. Absolute stillness—the wind was still, the sea was still, the ship was still. Vandiyadevan stared out at the sea, which was now as calm as a lake. But his heart was turbulent.

Then, all of a sudden, he extended both arms out to the sea, and screamed, 'Om hreem hraam vashattu!'

He took up his sword and whirled it round his head twice.

'Yes, yes, Samudra Raja wants a sacrifice! He craves blood, a double sacrifice! He asks for two evil souls, the kind that would attack men in their sleep! If we satisfy his hunger, he will let this ship sail upon his body, he says! Come, come fast, and lay out your heads for me to feed him!'

Ravidasan stared at Vandiyadevan, stunned. Then, he burst into insane laughter. 'Thambi, what is wrong with you?' he asked. 'What are you playing at?'

'Anna[1]! This isn't playing, this is a prophecy! When I was bound to the pole downstairs, I fell asleep from exhaustion, and began to dream. Well, it wasn't so much a dream as a vision. An enormous blue spirit, made of the sea and sky stitched together, appeared before me. It said something, and I couldn't quite make out the words. But I understand now. That was Samudra Raja, asking for the lives of two Kali devotees who are skilled in mantra-tantra. If I don't quench his thirst for blood, he will not let this ship sail. The six Arab bodies don't contain enough blood to satisfy him. Come, quick, now!' Vandiyadevan said, raising his sword as if to execute someone.

Ravidasan and the Devaraalan exchanged a look.

'Thambi, I've never met as skilled a storyteller as you,' Ravidasan said, finally.

'Oh, you don't believe me? You think I'm weaving a tall tale here? Samudra Raja! Won't you tell them yourself?'

Perhaps Samudra Raja heard him cry out. Perhaps he chose to respond. But, right on cue, a ripple passed through the sea and the waters began to shiver and shudder for as far as the eye could see. Thousands upon thousands of little waves rose and fell. All this happened in the space of a moment.

The next moment, each wave turned into foam. Bubbles frothed along the sea, as it churned in a fury. But what a beautiful sight it was, like a sea full of white flowers being teased into dance by a gentle breeze!

Yes, a gentle breeze, a pleasant cool breeze ... it caressed the ship on its way and passed them by. A shock of joy shuddered through the ship, and also through Vandiyadevan's body, soaked from the heat.

Ravidasan and the Devaraalan rolled about with laughter.

'Thambi! Samudra Raja has chosen to answer you! We must now ready ourselves for the sacrifice!' Ravidasan said, wiping away tears of mirth.

Vandiyadevan was disturbed by both the sea's unexpected response to his call and Ravidasan's amusement at it all.

What was this, now? The foam had dissolved! The waves had disappeared. The sea was now all flat again, flat as a metal sheet. Had it really stirred, or had he imagined it all? Or was Ravidasan truly a mantravadi?

'Did you see, thambi? The sky is responding to the sea!' Ravidasan said, pointing towards the south-west.

And there, in the direction he pointed, right along the horizon, where the blue of the sky met the green of the sea, was a grey cloud. And at the tip of the grey cloud, like a flame at the end of a matchstick, was a bright red spot. Vandiyadevan wouldn't have paid much attention to this phenomenon on any other day. What was so astounding about a raincloud on the horizon? But something about the timing of the sighting troubled our hero.

But then he fortified himself. He couldn't fall into the mantravadi's trap. The man was trying to manipulate him, find his weaknesses. No, he would put on a brave face.

He looked with wide eyes at Ravidasan and the Devaraalan, and then said, 'Oh, so both the sea and sky have spoken! Let us not delay the sacrifice. Please, do the honours!'

'Appane. Before we lay ourselves down on your sacrificial slab, we wish to pray to our kuladeivam, our clan deity. Would you grant us a quarter of a naazhigai?' Ravidasan asked.

'Sure, pray away, and then come. Don't try your tantra-mantra tricks with me, none of it will work,' Vandiyadevan said.

'We'll be back before you know it. See, we're even leaving our weapons here,' Ravidasan said.

The two men lowered their weapons on to the deck, and then went to the other side.

Vandiyadevan did need some time to recover. The sudden changes in the sea and then the sky had left him with a sense of foreboding. His body felt numb. He had to be able to think straight and act fast. If need be, he would kill both those lowlives with a single stroke. But would his arm have the strength to lift the sword when the time came? Why did he feel so drained? He had to use this time to talk himself into recovering his physical and mental strength.

He glanced towards the south-west again. The cloud had grown in size. The flame on its tip had dullened slightly. The cloud now seemed to be part of a cluster. Yes, there were rain clouds, rising higher and higher. The breeze began to blow again. The waters stirred too. Little waves danced on the surface of the sea. The wind seemed to have picked up. The ship moved slightly.

What was that other sound, the sound he heard over the rustle of the wind and the lapping of the waves? Where had Ravidasan and his friend gone? Those two must be up to something. Vandiyadevan turned around. He could not see them. Well, that was no surprise. They had crossed to the other side of the deck, and were hidden by the mast and its sails.

Ah! He knew that sound! Oars steering a boat! Vandiyadevan ran to the other side of the ship, and got the shock of his life. He had never expected this. He had thought the two men had asked for some time to come up with a plan to mollify him, but he had never imagined that they could have a raft stowed away on the other side of the deck. The raft was in the water now, and the two men were rowing away from the ship.

Ravidasan saw Vandiyadevan and laughed. 'Thambi! We don't intend to sacrifice our lives to the Samudra Raja, you see!'

Vandiyadevan realised his predicament at that moment. He was now all alone on this enormous ship. His former captors were making for the safety of land, having abandoned him ... on a ship he did not know how to sail. He had no clue where the ship was in relation to the shore, even. He did not know in which direction or for how long he would have to travel to find land anywhere! And those two had left him behind.

'Paavigale! Why didn't you take me with you?' he cried out.

'But how can we deprive Samudra Raja of a sacrifice, thambi?' Ravidasan called back, as the raft sailed away from the ship.

Vandiyadevan contemplated jumping into the sea and swimming to the raft. No, he wasn't the best swimmer. Even the idea of jumping off the ship made him feel sick. Even if he were to overcome his fears and jump, even if he were to overcome his incompetence and reach the raft, how could he be sure of the welcome he would get from those two? They had revealed their identities and their plans to him. They knew that he had no intention of ever joining forces with them. What if they knocked him out with an oar? He couldn't really take them on while he was flailing in the water, could he?

Well, let them go, let them go to hell! He was better off all alone on this enormous ship than sharing a raft with those monsters! He had escaped every predicament in which life had thrown him—or, in which he had thrown himself—by the grace of God, and he would escape this one too. The very same God would find a way to save him. Let Ravidasan and the Devaraalan go where they would!

But had he done the right thing in letting them get away alive? Where would they end up? What conspiracies might they hatch? What further attempts would they make on the prince's life? Well, he had to trust in God. What else could he do?

If only he could be reunited with the prince! Speaking of whom ... the prince hadn't really done right by him! Why hadn't he taken Vandiyadevan into confidence? Why had he run away with Poonguzhali on the elephant, all by himself, when he could have easily had Vandiyadevan join them? Right after his reunion with the prince, Vandiyadevan would demand an answer.

'Is this the *snehadharma* of your hallowed, ancient clan? Is this how the Chozhas treat their friends?' he would ask.

Would that opportunity arise? Would he ever meet the prince again? Whyever not? The senapati and Azhvarkadiyaan had seen him make for the ship. Surely, they would do something about it? They would tell the prince the moment they met him, wouldn't they?

Even as these thoughts ran through his mind, Vandiyadevan realised that the raft was now far, far away. How had they rowed so fast? No, it wasn't just the raft. The ship had started moving too. The waves were rising higher. And there was more ... what was this, darkness had descended on a part of the sea, right in the middle of the day!

Vandiyadevan looked towards the south-west again. The clouds now covered the sky, stretching far into the west. And they were moving fast, flying at breakneck speed. The sun was halfway through his descent into the west, but the clouds smothered him before he could complete his journey. And the skies were imposing themselves on the sea too, the dark clouds reflected in the waters and turning them grey. He could no longer tell where the sky ended and the sea began.

The clouds were now overhead. And now, they were spreading out to the east!

Vandiyadevan tried to gauge in which direction the ship was moving. He could not tell. As far as the eye could see, there was no land. The gentle rustle of the wind had now turned into a roar. And the waves were rising higher every moment. The flaps of the sails slammed into each other. The rods and sticks that had been stored on the ship clattered against each other, and sounded like a thousand doors banging shut. Vandiyadevan looked at the sails. He realised that the ship was not headed in any single direction, but was turning round and round.

He had heard of whirlwinds. Perhaps he was caught in one such storm now! Vandiyadevan could tell that it was important to furl the sails. But how could one man do this? It was a ten-man job! At least a four-man job! There was no way he alone could manage it. He had no choice but to leave it to fate.

The fate that awaited the ship was evident before long. It would be tossed about on the waves, and eventually swallowed by the sea. The only question was whether it would be swallowed whole, or break into bits before that happened. And there was no question about his own fate.

Death at sea.

The astrologer in Kudandai[2] hadn't said a word about this. Not a hint. He could see the future, could he? If only Vandiyadevan were to meet him again … ha! Meet him again! Vandiyadevan wasn't ever going to meet a soul again. Not a living soul, at least.

Something heavy fell on Vandiyadevan's shoulder. Pebbles seemed to be raining on the deck of the ship. How they shone, like little marbles! But how were pebbles falling from the sky?

They continued to fall, on his head and shoulders and back. At first, he felt pain at the point where each one hit him, and then the spot felt cool. He looked at the pebbles on the deck. What, they were melting! Ah, so these were hailstones! He had heard of such a phenomenon, but never seen it before. And now, he was going to experience it all! He couldn't help feeling excited about the coming storm.

He touched the melting rocks on the deck. Ah, what a strange sensation! They felt like fire against his skin, but then the heat turned into water and left his palms tingling. Then, as suddenly as the hailstorm had begun, it ended, barely half a naazhigai later.

And then, the rain began to pour. Vandiyadevan watched the water hit the deck and slide off the surface to join the sea. What wonderful architects Chozha Naadu could boast of, he thought. However hard the ship was hit by rain, it would not sink. They had ensured that the water would run off into the sea. And so, the vessel would not go under unless the hull of the ship broke, for some reason.

He was emboldened by this observation. And then he remembered that the door to the room in which he had been bound earlier might be open. That would allow water to enter the inside of the ship. He ran to check. The door was slapping against the frame in the high winds. He rushed to close it. He drew the bolt to ensure the door would remain shut.

If the rain and wind on board became too much to bear, he could take shelter in this room. He would leave the rest to God. How foolish of Ravidasan and the Devaraalan to jump off such a sturdy ship and expose themselves to the vagaries of the sea on a flimsy raft! That said, the raft was a work of art too. However hard the wind blew and the rain fell, it would not sink. And even if it were to fall apart, those murderers could hold on to one of its constituent pieces of wood and stay afloat until help arrived, or until they could navigate to the shore. They would likely land somewhere near Kodikkarai.

And from Kodikkarai, Vandiyadevan's heart and mind leapt to Pazhaiyarai. How would the emperor's cherished daughter get to know of his predicament? Who would tell her that he had drowned while trying to fulfil his promise to her? Would the sea tell her? Or would a gust of wind from these parts blow her way, carrying the sights and sounds it had absorbed? If he was going to die anyway, he ought to have died before he met that incredible woman! He had had plenty of opportunity to die a hero's death in war. If only that had happened, he would have gone to Heaven before he had encountered heaven on earth. How cruel the gods were to allow him a peek at that heaven before consigning him to the pits of hell!

The wind was getting stronger, and the sea rougher. The sails of the ship were howling like ghosts in grief. The sun had waved goodbye a long time ago, and the darkness was deeper than the blackest of nights. How was such a thing possible? Well, it was.

All of a sudden, a bolt of lightning tore through the sky, diving from one end to the other. And after that, he couldn't see a thing. Blacker than black, he thought, as a deafening roar of thunder followed the lightning. The sea was torn into shreds, and the axis of the world shifted. This blackness was eviscerated by another bolt of lightning. But this one lingered. It lit up the sky, teased all the colours of the rainbow from the clouds and set the sea aflame. And then it disappeared. The thunder that followed ... the universe[3] was splitting, there was no doubt about it. Ammamma! More lightning and more thunder.

How had the sky not actually fallen upon his head, he wondered, even as it did fall upon his head! And with that began the pralayam[4] that would end this world.

No, this was not rain. It was a sea trying to break the ceiling over this one. And as that ceiling split, the sea above poured into the one below. The waves danced as if possessed. In the intervals of lightning, Vandiyadevan thought he saw the peaks of mountains floating in those waters. Yes, mountains made of water. And then the wind blew faster than ever. Vayu Bhagavan was lifting those mountains and hurling them into the sky, playing with his celestial friends, who threw those mountains of water right back ... onto the ship.

Sea overhead and sea underfoot, mountains of water on either side and a wind that wouldn't let up. Yet, this incredible ship only spun round and round, without getting swallowed up by the raging elements. But how long could it withstand this assault? This moment, or the next, or the one after, the ship would have to give up. And take Vandiyadevan to his watery grave.

But the thought didn't depress him. It would be a death for the ages, a grand farewell to this world. He felt inspired by the thought, and his heart leapt with joy. There was a symphony in the air, with the screaming of the wind and the heaving of the water and the drumbeats of thunder. This was primal music, and he was part of it. He shouted, louder than the gale, 'Haa! Haa! Haaaaa!' and laughed.

He was going to see this through. He was going to see it all, before he perished in glory. He bound himself to the mast of the ship. As the ship spun, the sails spun too, as did Vandiyadevan. He went round and round and round. He couldn't tell for how long. It could have been seconds, it could have been aeons. He had transcended all sense of time.

And then, the wind began to slow down. The rain turned into a drizzle. The thunder and lightning stopped. The sea was a black expanse now.

Vandiyadevan who had shut his eyes tight to shield them from the brightness of the lightning and had pressed his hands to his ears to dull the unbearable din of thunder now opened his eyes and freed his ears.

Had he actually survived a storm at sea? And such a tempest too? Had God saved him yet again? Would he see the princess in Pazhaiyarai again? In this lifetime, not the next one? Would he meet the prince, too, and hold him in a tight embrace?

No, he must not get ahead of himself. Who knew where the ship was? How could he be sure he would reach land at some point? Even if the ship survived, who could tell whether he himself would?

How many perils awaited him?

As if to answer his questions, a bolt of lightning cut the sky neatly in half, and then threw the two parts aside. A thousand suns now shone into his eyes.

One could see in the dark, even. But one could not think in such blinding light. Had he lost his eyes to the lightning, he wondered, even as he had lost his ears to the most tremendous noise he had ever heard. This was not thunder, this was Indra's thunderbolt, the vajrayudha tearing through one ear drum to enter his head and tearing out the other to exit.

For a while, Vandiyadevan could not open his eyes. His ears were ringing. Through his closed eyelids, he sensed a strange new brightness. And the ringing subsided into a different sound, a strange crackling. The sound of a forest on fire, the sound of trees going up in flames ...

Vandiyadevan forced his eyes open. He looked up and saw ... fire. The tip of the canvas of the skysail was on fire. Now he understood why the thousand suns had blazed so bright and why the thunder had seemed so near. Because the vajrayudha had hit the ship. And the sail was on fire. Where two of the pancha bhoota[5] had failed to destroy the ship, a third had taken over. Water and wind had not beaten the Chozha ship. And so, Varuna and Vayu had outsourced their task to Agni.

22

# THE BROKEN BOAT

Once he realised that the sails were on fire, Vandiyadevan knew there was no chance of the ship surviving the storm. And, therefore, no chance of his surviving it either. But the thought didn't sadden him. He laughed louder than ever. He untied the rope with which he had bound himself to the mast. It would be a pity to die by fire in the middle of the ocean. The cold water would make for a rather more pleasant deathbed.

He didn't want to waste the little time he had left to live. Now that there was light to see by—with the fire making as handy a flame as any—he could take in the beautiful sight of the dancing waves. This was going to be his samadhi after all. It was said that people who died before their time roamed the sites of their deaths as spirits. Would his spirit circle this spot forever then? Would it float on the breeze or swim in the water? And if the whirlwinds hit again, would his ghost spin too?

Aha, who knew, perhaps the princess would sail on a grand ship upon this very sea? The sailors would point out the spot where Vandiyadevan had sunk with his ship. Those lovely eyes, shaped like the tip of a spear, would spill little pearls of tears. Would his spirit, observing all this from close quarters, be able to wipe her wet cheeks?

The ship now crested an enormous wave. In the light of the fire, he could see for a great distance. The sea was as black marble. The flame at the top of the mast was a ball of fire in the water. Before Vandiyadevan could marvel at this exquisite sight, something else demanded his attention.

Some distance away was another ship. The tiger flag was flying on it.

Was there no end to the wonders he would witness? Surely, the ship must be commandeered by Prince Arulmozhi Varmar? He must have set out in search of his friend! Vandiyadevan's instinct told him this was, indeed, the case.

As our readers must know, Parthibendran's ship had been caught in the same storm that had hit Vandiyadevan's. However, it had a full crew of experienced sailors, who knew how to handle a storm at sea. They had furled the sails the moment the wind had picked up. They had helmed the ship, steering it so it did not have to fight the full force of the storm.

One moment, the ship would tilt so dangerously that the passengers were convinced it was going to sink. The next, it would have righted itself, thanks to its crew. The planks and beams that held the ship together had withstood the assault of those mountainous waves. They had held their own against Samudra Raja, who had thrown the ship about like he was playing a ball game with his friends, and the whirlwinds, which had spun it like a top. The skies had opened, and the waters had tried to press the ship down into the sea and drown it, but the craftsmen of Chozha Naadu had fortified the vessel against everything nature could throw at it, and the sailors of Tamizhagam had played their part too.

'I've seen whirlwinds and tempests that are far more violent than this, and survived them all,' the kalapati had said. 'There is no cause for concern on that account.'

However, there *was* another cause for concern, and he told the prince and Parthibendran what that was.

'The clouds have blocked the sun entirely. And the rain has formed a screen of water. As if this weren't enough, the waves are so high one can barely see ahead. Even if the ship we're pursuing comes close, we won't be able to see it. Naturally, that ship will be about as helpless as we are. If the two are to clash, they will both break. And all of us aboard will be done for. So, the whirlwinds don't pose the greatest danger.

It is the fact that we cannot see around us that is the real peril,' the kalapati said.

The prince was already aware of this. And he had already been walking to every corner of the deck, squinting into the distance, hoping his sharp eyes could discern the other ship before it was too late. Every time lightning flashed, he scanned the sea, his heart in his mouth. The messenger his sister had sent was now at the mercy of savage Arabs and murdering mantravadis. And they were all at the mercy of this wind storm. What if they did not succeed in spotting the ship? And what if they did see it, only to find that all its occupants had drowned? What if the ships did clash, as the kalapati had warned?

What a joke that would be! Who would carry his message to the emperor if both he and Vandiyadevan were to drown together? He couldn't trust a family secret to Parthibendran. The Pallava scion would scoff at it, without understanding the seriousness of that long-ago tryst.

No, he must not think of such things, the prince told himself. He had never failed at anything on which he had set his mind. Would he fail now? No, never.

Would Samudra Raja allow Ponni's beloved prince to know failure or harm?

Arulmozhi Varmar kept his eyes peeled for the ship, his sight tearing through the darkness and the rain. He saw the bolt of lightning and had to close his eyes, and the sound of thunder made him clap his hands to his ears. When he opened his eyes again, the light had changed. The bolt of lightning had transformed into a flame. There it was! A ship with its sails unfurled, in the middle of a frenzied dance on the water! The skysail was on fire, as was the mast. And there was a man tied to the mast! What was this? Oh, god, it was his dear friend, that reckless youth, Vandiyadevan! Why was he all alone on the ship? What had become of everyone else? Well, there was no time to waste on speculation.

The prince knew right away what he had to do.

He was not the only one who had spotted the other ship.

A chorus of 'There!' rose from nearly all the men aboard, their overjoyed voices drowning out the sound of the raging winds.

The prince marched up to the boat fastened to the side of the ship and then looked back at the sailors. 'Which of you will come with me?' he demanded.

The sailors, who had guessed what he intended to do, were stunned. And yet, they jostled each other to volunteer.

Parthibendran and the kalapati tried to dissuade him.

'Ilavarase! What insane idea is this? How can anyone sail a boat on these waters? And how will you save a man from a burning ship? If you insist on making a pointless attempt, why must it be you yourself who undertakes it, when any one of us would risk his life for you?' Parthibendran asked. 'Please, let one of us go in your stead!'

'Be warned! I will never forgive anyone who tries to stop me now,' the prince said, in a regal tone that would brook no argument. Even as he said the words, he unmoored the boat and lowered it to the sea. 'I only need two men. Come!'

The rest of the men watched helplessly as the prince and two sailors got on the boat. It rushed off along the churning waves, teetering dangerously. The three men plied the oars to make it go faster. They were nearing the burning ship.

By this time, the fire had caught on. It had climbed down the mast and swallowed the topsail. Vandiyadevan stood, as if in a trance. He had seen the ship, and the boat that was making its way towards him. But he was frozen in place, as if he had forgotten that he had to play an active part in his own rescue.

'Jump! Jump into the sea!' the prince cried.

Vandiyadevan did not hear him. He looked at the boat blankly.

This was it. If they waited any longer, the entire deck would catch fire. The ship would be consumed by the flames, as would Vandiyadevan.

Again, the prince knew right away what he had to do. He reached for the long rope stocked in the boat for just such an emergency, secured one end firmly around his waist, and handed the other end over to the two sailors. He then jumped into the sea.

The waters that had toyed with the boat now toyed with the prince. They tossed him up into the skies one moment, and sank him into the bowels of the earth the next. Even so, the prince did not waver. He swam resolutely in the right direction, edging closer to the burning ship with every stroke.

And then a giant wave tore through the sea. It could have swallowed the prince whole. But this was a kind-hearted wave, come to aid him in his mission. It carried the prince gently and deposited him neatly on the deck of the burning ship.

The moment he saw the prince, Vandiyadevan let out a cry and jumped towards him. The prince wound an arm around his friend's neck and shouted, 'Hold on to me! Don't let go! Come, let's go!'

With that, he dived from the burning ship into the water, taking Vandiyadevan with him.

The sailors kept the oars aside and began to pull at the rope. The prince watched in relief as the boat loomed closer. It was no easy task to get on it even when they were right by it. He had to fight the tide, and carry the weight of a motionless Vandiyadevan. Every moment felt like an age to him.

Again and again, he would feel he had a safe grip, right before he lost it. Each time, he thought he had lost his friend for good, and it took his all to hang on. After several rounds of this, the prince was all but ready to give up, when another giant wave stepped in. It carried the men right up to the rim of the boat, and the sailors pulled them on board.

'Take up the oars! Row fast!' the prince cried.

He had just looked at the burning ship, and realised that it was about to break. The turbulence caused by the sinking ship would suck the boat into the waters. They might capsize. Worse, once the fire went out, they wouldn't be able to spot their own ship.

Aha! There, the ship had begun to sink.

It was a glorious sight, the fire that was raging through the wood being swallowed by the water. And as the prince had expected, the suction it generated was terrifying. The waves rose to the very sky.

Their little boat managed to stay afloat. But it turned pitch dark once the fire went out. Where were they? Where was Parthibendran's ship? Were they getting closer to the ship or moving further away? They had no idea. And both situations presented danger. If they got too close to the other ship, they might strike it, to their detriment; or the wake would pull them underwater. And if they got too far ... well, need one ask? What could a little boat do in the middle of an angry sea? Oh, Samudra Raja! This is the son of your beloved Ponni river. Aren't you duty-bound to save his life?

The caprices of Vayu Bhagavan were strange. The wind died down as suddenly as it had risen. And, as he tore off to new horizons, he tormented the sea on his way.

Well, so that was the end of the whirlwind. But the turbulence of the water was not going away any time soon. It would take a whole night and a whole day for it to subside. And the turbulence would spread in all four directions. The seawaters would consume the wide beaches of Kodikkarai. They would break the shores of Nagapattinam. They would spread to Kangesan Thurai and Tirikonamalai. They would have their way with Mathottam and Rameshwaram.

The boat on which the prince and his companions sat was bouncing around in the waters. The oarsmen had given up. What was the point of steering a boat when they did not know which way they must go? The wind and rain had tired themselves out. The thunder and lightning were gone. But the waves were determined to vent their rage on everything that came their way.

Even as the boat was struggling through the waves, an entirely unexpected peril came their way. It got closer and closer, unsighted. And then, there it was! A part of the mast that had not completely burnt down had contrived to outlive the sinking ship. And now, it was right by the boat. They could not see it for the dark, until it was right upon them.

The prince's eyes widened in horror and he shouted, 'The oars! The oars! Ply the oars!'

He had not even closed his mouth before the mast lodged itself under the boat, which split with a loud *padaar*! First, it broke into two, and then into fragments.

'Don't worry!' the prince cried to his friend. 'The mast is sturdier than this boat. Hold on to it!'

23

# SONG OF SOLACE

Let us go back in time now, before the storm had hit, when the prince had insisted that he would go in search of his friend, and then left on a boat.

The men left behind at the estuary of the Thondaimanaru hadn't taken their eyes off the boat until the prince had reached Parthibendran's ship. Once he was safely aboard, the boat he had taken to the ship returned to shore.

Senapati Boothi Vikrama Kesari's relief and joy were evident on his face.

'God is on our side, there's no doubt,' he mumbled to himself. 'The prince has the sangu-chakra[1] emblems on his hands ... how could God be but on our side? Parthibendran will escort him safely to Kanchi. All I have left to do is gather my armies and head for Thanjavur.'

He then turned to Azhvarkadiyaan, who was standing nearby, and realised he had spoken aloud.

Tirumalai must have heard everything. 'Vaishnavane!' he said. 'You've been standing quietly all this while, have you? Listening to me? Well, so what? Is there anything to which the prime minister's trusted informant isn't privy? What are your plans now? Will you come with me to Mathottam?'

'No, aiya, I'm yet to complete another task the prime minister has assigned to me.'

'And what might that be?'

Azhvarkadiyaan looked at a point some distance away, where the Oomai Rani and Poonguzhali stood.

'Does it have to do with those women?' the senapati asked.

'One of them, yes. The prime minister told me that if I were to chance upon a mute woman who fits a certain description, I was to convince her to return to Thanjavur with me.'

'Some task he's assigned you! He might as well have asked you to catch hold of a whirlwind and bring it back. Just about as easy as getting that woman to do your bidding, I'd say. Who is she? Do you know anything at all about her? She is so fond of our prince, and I have no idea who she might be.'

'I know she's mute, and that she was born deaf. Contrary to your view, I believe it would be far easier to catch hold of a whirlwind than get her to do my bidding. However, I'm bound by duty to give it a shot.'

'It appears she is friends with that boatwoman. Look at them talking through signs! Call that girl here. I have to warn her about something.'

Azhvarkadiyaan went up to the women and told Poonguzhali the senapati wanted to see her. She conveyed this to the Oomai Rani, and came back with him.

'Look here, young woman ... you're a clever one. You came at just the right time, with a piece of important news. The Chozha dynasty owes you for this good turn. I will never forget what you have done. You will be rewarded at the right time,' the senapati said.

'Thank you, aiya, but I have no interest in a reward,' Poonguzhali said politely.

'So what if you have no interest in a reward? It won't stop me from ensuring we've paid you for your service. Let all this commotion die down. And then ... and then ... I'll select a warrior from the Chozha army myself, and get you married to him. He can't be any ordinary soldier, he must be Bheemasena himself, no? Or, you'll do him in!' the senapati said, laughing.

Poonguzhali kept her eyes on the ground. She was seething. But she held her anger in check. There was no point in getting into a conflict with this old man on a warpath.

'But you must keep this in mind—you might have done the prince a good turn, but do not presume that entitles you to a close camaraderie with him. Stick to casting your nets in the waters and catching your fish. Don't aspire to trap the prince, you hear me? Consider yourself warned, penne ... trying to get close to him again will only put you in danger's way,' the senapati said. His tone was harsh, and he spat out his words. They hit Poonguzhali's ears like molten lead.

She ached to give it back word for word, insult for insult. But her throat was constricted. She couldn't find her voice. The molten lead flowed from her ears to her eyes, from which it spilled out as hot tears.

Without lifting her eyes off the ground, Poonguzhali turned on her heel and walked away from the shore, further into the island. She started off at a slow pace, and picked up speed as she walked. She turned to look at the Oomai Rani for a moment, and saw Azhvarkadiyaan trying to convey something to her. She wanted to walk away from them all. She wanted to go to a place where she would not meet another human being, ever. How nasty people were! Why would anyone speak such cruel words? If only everyone were mute!

After walking in the forest for a while, she reached the shore of the Thondaimanaru. She made for the spot where she had anchored her boat. She must get there quickly. Yes, she would climb into her boat and set out into the sea, all alone. She must go to a spot where no human voice could reach her, out in the middle of the ocean. She would keep her oars aside. The boat would float gently on the waves, and she would be a passive passenger on the craft. She would journey for all eternity on the infinite sea. That was the only way her thundering heart would slow to a normal beat. The hurt that the senapati's words had caused would abate. Her fury would give way to solace.

What had the old man said? 'Stick to casting your nets in the waters and catching your fish. Don't aspire to trap the prince, you hear me?'

She was casting a net to trap the prince, was she? *She?* Chhi, chhi! How perverse the old man was! The fish were far gentler, kinder souls than humans. They didn't mouth such ugly utterances. They whiled away their days, swimming underwater and playing on the surface of the sea. All they knew was joy. They had no worries, no sorrows. Aha, why hadn't she been born a fish? She could have spent her entire life in the water, as she did now, only without the anxieties and anger and heartache and hurt and betrayal and brooding that she was feeling right now. There would be no one, then, trying to come between her and the prince, to insult her and hurl such venom at her. No, no, there was no guarantee of peace in the life of a fish either. These violent humans would cast nets to trap her. If they saw two fish in love, they might even go to the trouble of separating them just for kicks. Nasty, nasty, nasty people!

Her rage fuelled her legs, and she reached her boat by sundown. Thankfully, it was safely anchored in the same spot. The boat was her best friend, her most trusted companion, her source of solace, her safe place. This was the tiny space that was her own, that sheltered her from the callousness and treachery of this world. She should be grateful no one had stolen it.

Everything and everyone could go to hell, she thought. The old man could guard the prince all he wanted. Let him put the prince in a cage and hang that Kodumbalur princess around his neck. Who cared? She had her boat, she could ply the oars, she had strength in her arms and the vast expanse of the ocean to welcome her.

*Samudra Raja! You will look out for your daughter, won't you? You won't betray me like everyone else has, will you? You won't make the title that the prince has bestowed on me with his beloved, smiling mouth false, will you? I will always be Samudra Kumari, your Samudra Kumari, won't I?*

Poonguzhali got into the boat, and rowed it out towards the sea. She was rowing downstream, and it didn't take her long to reach the estuary of the Thondaimanaru. Then, she was practically on the ocean. Soon enough, she realised that a storm was about to hit the sea. She knew the signs. The previous night, there had been an ash-coloured rim around the moon. The day had been unbearably humid and suffocatingly airless. Not one leaf on a tree had moved. There, towards the south-west, she could see dark clouds gather. There was no doubt about it, a wind storm was about to hit them. Well, the sea would be a beautiful sight as the waves rose. But it would not do to be caught in the tempest. The wisest option would be to row to Bhoota Theevu and wait it out. She would have a view of the sea in all its terrible beauty. Once the wind had died down and the waves had lost their fervour, she would take the boat out again, and row all the way to Kodikkarai. What was the hurry, anyway? The ship must have reached Kodikkarai by now. Thankfully, it would not have got caught in the storm. The prince would have reached land safely. He might have chosen to go to Mamallapuram instead of Kodikkarai too. What did it matter to her, either way? Just as long as he hadn't been caught in the storm. It was enough for her that he was safe.

Remember, reader, at this time Poonguzhali had no idea that the prince's ship had been unable to sail because the wind had come to a complete halt just before the storm. She assumed it would have reached its destination.

*Stick to casting your nets in the waters and catching your fish. Don't aspire to trap the prince, you hear me?*

The senapati's words echoed in her ears and caused an ache in her chest. She felt no desire to reach Kodikkarai. She might as well stay and watch the storm from Bhoota Theevu. The island was not far from the estuary, and she was there within a naazhigai. She arrived on land right as the storm hit the sea.

She dragged the boat onto land and secured it. She then made for a Buddhist stupa of which she knew. For a while, she stayed in an alcove, sheltered from the wind and rain. But she could not stay put for long. She wanted to see Vayu Bhagavan's awe-inspiring fury for herself. She climbed the steps of the stupa and went right to the top.

Nature was in sync with her mind. The coconut trees that had been born and grown into adulthood on this island stood wailing and tearing their hair, dancing in frenzy as the demons would dance around Samhara Murti[2] when Doomsday arrived. The waves dwarfed the coconut trees, reaching Himalayan heights, only to disintegrate into bubbles. The howling of the wind, the dancing of the waves and the breaking of thunderclaps made one think that celestial bodies were colliding with each other. The sky was falling. Bolts of lightning flashed in the sky, and showed the possessed coconut trees and the gigantic waves in all their glory, only to plunge the world into darkness as they disappeared.

Poonguzhali stood watching for a long time. Her body shook with the wind. Her hairdo came undone and her tresses flew in the air even as rain soaked her clothes. The thunder tore through her eardrums and the lightning blinded her. But none of it mattered to her. She stood, motionless. It was as if the universe was staging a play just for her. She couldn't take her eyes off the spectacle.

Every now and again, a vision of Prince Arulmozhi Varmar appeared before her eyes. He must be resting in a palace, after having reached Kodikkarai right before the storm. Why, perhaps he was in his parents' palace? Or in the royal palace in Nagapattinam? What if he had still been at sea when the storm had hit? Well, so what if he had? The ship was a formidable vessel, and no tempest would harm it. He would be surrounded by experienced sailors and men willing to lay down their lives to protect him. Would he remember her? Was he, by any chance, wondering about her safety? Would he be worried for her? No, of course not. All his thoughts would be with Vandiyadevan. Perhaps he would spare some thought for the Kodumbalur princess to whom his sister had taken a shine. Why would he bother about the boatwoman he had met so briefly?

Poonguzhali spent most of the night watching the storm, and finally made her way down the steps of the stupa and into her alcove. She dozed off, and had all sorts of dreams. In one, she was out at sea, casting her net. The prince was caught in it. She woke with a start. What madness! She went back to sleep, and this time, dreamt that she and the prince had turned into two fish, swimming side by side for all eternity.

When she finally rose, well into the day, it was to the calm after the storm. No thunder, no lightning. No rain, even. She made her way to the shore. The waves were still high, although nowhere near as terrifying as they had been the previous night. The damage the storm had wreaked on the island was evident in the enormous trees that lay on the ground, uprooted. There were those with gnarled trunks, which had stood the test of time but had not been able to withstand the storm.

As Poonguzhali stood, taking in the sight, something strange appeared among the waves—it looked like a catamaran floating about on the water. It was approaching the shore, but the sea had its way with it, teasing it, before allowing it to reach the sand. It was then that Poonguzhali noticed that the catamaran had an occupant.

She ran towards the catamaran, and saw that the man inside was half-dead. He had been tied to the raft. She undid the ropes and did her best to revive him. When he was able to talk, he told her that he was from a fishing village on the Eezham coast. He had been out fishing with a companion when the storm had hit. His friend had died at sea. As for him, he had died and been reborn, he said.

He had something else to say too.

'Last evening, there was a lull in the storm. It was pitch dark, and then there was a bolt of lightning that blinded us. But in that flash of light, we saw two ships—one was on fire. We could see figures hurrying about on deck. We saw their silhouettes against the fire, and were transfixed by the terrible sight. Eventually, that ship sank. The other one disappeared into the dark.'

As she heard the words, it struck Poonguzhali that the prince might have been aboard one of the ships. No, no, that was impossible. There were just so many ships at sea. Who knew which ones these were? The prince was safe, she had no doubt about that. Yes, he was safe. But those people who had been caught in the fire ... perhaps some of them had jumped off the ship? Perhaps they were still in water? Perhaps, like this fisherman, they had floundered about in the water and then caught hold of whatever they could find to keep themselves afloat? Some might still be out at sea, waiting for help. She should row her boat out to sea and look for survivors? What was this life for, if one didn't spend it helping those in need?

That was it. The moment the thought struck her, Poonguzhali's legs made their way to her boat and her hands let it out to sea. Her strong arms worked hard, so the oars would break through the rowdy waves by the shore. Once she was in deeper waters, the going was easier. Her practised arms rowed easily. The boat danced across the waves.

Poonguzhali's heart was full. The song she usually sang when she was at sea rose to her throat and soon, her lovely voice broke through the noise of the waves and the notes of the song resonated across the water, this time with some changes:

*Alaikkadal kondalikkaiyile*
*Agakkadaldaan kalippadumen?*
*Nilamagalum tudikkayile*
*Nenjagandaan tulluvaden?*
*Idi idiththu endisaiyum*

*Vedipadum avvelayile*
*Nadanakkalai vallavarpol*
*Nattiyandaan aaduvaden?*

*While the sea froths and fumes*
*Why do waves of joy rise within?*
*While the earth is in torment,*
*Why is my heart so full of cheer?*
*Even as thunder splits the sky*
*And skews the paths of stars*
*How does my spirit feel moved to dance*
*Like a virtuoso to its beat?*

~*~

And what about the prince and Vandiyadevan?

They were holding on to the fallen mast and letting themselves float about. It was only one night, but to Vandiyadevan it seemed to last aeons. He could no longer recall a time when he had not been at sea, clinging on for dear life to a piece of wood. He had lost all hope and all desire. He was ready to die. Every time a wave pulled them up like toys and dropped them to its trough, he was sure he was taking his last breath. Every time he survived this, it surprised him.

Every now and again, he looked at the prince and lamented. 'My impulsive nature has brought you to this ... I've put you in peril because I am the way I am.'

And every time, the prince comforted him. 'There are people who have survived after three or four days at sea after a storm.'

'How many days has it been since we fell into the water?' Vandiyadevan asked.

'Not even one whole day,' the prince said.

'Lies! Lies! It must have been many, many days!' Vandiyadevan cried.

Not long after, a new problem arose. His throat felt dry. He was aching with thirst. There was water as far as the eye could see, and yet not a drop to drink. It was torture.

When he whined to the prince, Arulmozhi Varmar said, 'Hold on for a while. It will soon be light, and we'll be able to swim to the shore.'

After a while, Vandiyadevan could no longer bear it. 'This is torture, aiya! I cannot take this. Please untie these ropes. Let me drown and die.'

The prince tried to talk sense into him, but Vandiyadevan was in a frenzy. He began to undo the ropes that bound him. The prince crawled towards him, and then punched him twice, right on the head. Vandiyadevan lost consciousness.

When he came to, dawn had broken. The sea was slightly calmer. The sun must have risen somewhere, but he could not see it.

The prince looked at him with affection and said, 'Thozha![3] We must be near the shore. I saw the fronds of a coconut tree not so long ago. Have some patience.'

'Ilavarase! Don't let me hold you back. Leave me, and save yourself,' Vandiyadevan said.

'No, I won't leave you. Don't lose heart. You'll see, we ... oh! What is this? Aha! It sounds like someone singing!' the prince said.

The two of them listened, and they heard the words:

*Alaikkadal kondalikkayile*
*Agakkadaldaan kalippadumen?*

*While the sea froths and fumes*
*Why do waves of joy rise within?*

It was the song of solace. Vandiyadevan, who had lost most of his strength, found himself rejuvenated. His physical and mental exhaustion abated. The song filled him with joy.

'Ilavarase! That is Poonguzhali's voice! It has to be! She is rowing her boat here. We will live!' he cried.

Soon, they could see the boat. It came closer and closer.

~*~

Poonguzhali sat frozen. Could this really be happening?

She watched numbly as the prince untied the ropes that bound Vandiyadevan to the mast. He then leapt onto the boat, and pulled his friend on board too.

Poonguzhali was still frozen, the oars in her hands, still as a painting.

The story continues in
# BOOK 5
# DEATHLY SWORD

*An Extract*

# 13

## THE POISONED POTION

Vandiyadevan's heart nearly stopped at the sight of the Devaraalan in that place, at that time. The memory of his frenzied dance and terrifying words at the Kadambur Palace came to mind, as did the words he and Ravidasan had spoken to him as the ship had bounced about the waves helplessly during the storm. It was hard to tell how much of that was true, and how much imagined. But he was certain of this much—they were involved in some sort of terrible secret conspiracy. Just his luck, Vandiyadevan thought, to have run into one of them in the middle of nowhere. He wondered for a moment whether he should simply make a run for it, urging his horse to fly. He looked about himself to gauge his prospects. He could see fire in the distance. It must be a crematorium.

*A mortal body is now feeding that fire. When there was life in that body, how many ups and downs it must have seen! How many desires it must have been subject to, how many wishes must have tormented it! How many joys and how many sorrows it must have experienced! And yet, half a naazhigai will reduce all those desires and wishes and joys and sorrows into a fistful of ash. This is what will become of everyone born in this world. The grandest of kings and the poorest of paupers will one day turn into prey for this fire and end up as a fistful of ash,* Vandiyadevan thought.

His panic disappeared as suddenly as it had set in. What reason did he have to be afraid of this trickster? Clearly, the Devaraalan was here to tell him something. He might as well hear it. Had it been the Devaraalan who had left by the backdoor as Vandiyadevan had entered the forge, he wondered. Perhaps that incredible sword had been his? Vandiyadevan was sure he had seen the insignia of a fish near the grip of that sword. He might be able to glean some information if he could draw the Devaraalan into conversation.

And so, Vandiyadevan set a leisurely pace for his horse. The animal, too, seemed to be struggling with his freshly shod hooves. Vandiyadevan did not have the heart to urge the horse to go faster.

'How did you land up here, appa?' he asked.

'I should be the one asking that question,' the Devaraalan said. 'We left you on the ship in the middle of the sea, during a storm. How did you manage to escape?'

'You think you're the only one who knows mantras and magic? I'm not bad at it myself.'

'I'm glad to hear you believe in mantras and magic. I learnt from those very powers that you'd be wandering about all alone here. That's why I came ahead, to wait for you.'

'Why were you waiting? What business do you have with me?'

'Figure it out for yourself. Or, divine it with your magical powers.'

'You told me your secrets in the middle of the ocean. I don't know how much of what you said is fact and how much is fiction. But I've decided to forget it all. I don't plan on telling anyone what you said.'

'I have no worries on that account. The moment you so much as consider telling a soul what we told you, your tongue will be sliced off. You'll end up mute.'

A chill ran down Vandiyadevan's spine. He thought of the two mute women he had met in Thanjavur and Lanka. He kept up a casual pace for some time. Why was this creature following him? How was he to lose the Devaraalan? If only he could find a pit of quicksand, as he had in Kodikkarai! Or, perhaps, he could throw the man into the river? No, there would be little point. The current wasn't too swift, and there wasn't enough water to drown him. Of course, if all else failed, he had his sword in his scabbard.

'Thambi, it's obvious to me what you're thinking. But it won't work. What's the point of undertaking a fool's mission?'

Vandiyadevan wanted to change the subject. He needed to buy some time to get away from the Devaraalan. It might be a good idea to taunt him into a useful revelation.

'What happened to your comrade Ravidasan?'

The Devaraalan made a show of laughing and then said, 'You're the one who ought to know, right? Where is Ravidasan? You tell me.'

Vandiyadevan was startled. He ought not to have mentioned Ravidasan. He'd made a mistake. Had the Devaraalan met Ravidasan already, learnt what had passed and decided to put him to the test now, Vanidadevan wondered. Or ...

'Why, thambi, why are you silent? Won't you tell me where Ravidasan is? Well, that's all right. At least tell me this ... where is that boat girl, Poonguzhali?'

At this, Vandiyadevan reacted like a man who'd just stepped on a snake. He was afraid to say any more.

'Oh, so you won't tell me about her either. Well, never mind. Perhaps you have a solid reason for wanting to protect her. Why, you were singing a love song some time ago, weren't you? Is she the one the song is in honour of?'

'No, no, I swear that's not true!' Vandiyadevan cried.

'Why are you so flustered? And so angry?'

'All right, all right, there's no time to talk about all that. Why have you caught my horse by his reins now? Let go! I need to leave, I'm on an important mission!'

'But you haven't asked me what *my* mission is.'

'How can I ask when you won't let me get a word in edgeways?'

'Well, you see, this Mullaiyaru shore has a unique power. If you make a wish standing here, it will be granted right away.'

'I have no wish or desire,' replied Vandiyadevan.

'That's a lie! The person whom you had in mind while singing your love song wishes to see you. If you'd like, you can meet her.'

'When?'

'Tonight.'

'What nonsense!'

'No nonsense, thambi. There, look!' and the Devaraalan pointed in the distance.

Vandiyadevan could make out a vague outline in the distance. He squinted. It was a palanquin, a closed palanquin.

Now, dear readers, where have we seen that palanquin before? Why, it is the Pazhuvoor Ilaiya Rani's palanquin, isn't it? Is Nandini inside, you wonder. As did Vandiyadevan. He couldn't contain his curiosity.

He sped towards the palanquin on his horse. He could see the curtain, and it seemed to him that someone parted it slightly from inside.

Vandiyadevan leapt off his horse.

At the same time, an odd sound emanated from the Devaraalan's throat.

From the bushes around him, bodies began to emerge. Seven or eight men closed in on Vandiyadevan and pounced on him and gripped him so tightly he could not so much as move. They bound his feet and hands, and then tied a blindfold over his eyes. One of them grabbed Vandiyadevan's sword. They then threw him into the palanquin. The palanquin began to move fast. The Devaraalan led the way, and the rest of the men followed, some carrying the palanquin and the others walking by it. One of the men led Vandiyadevan's horse.

All this had happened in a fraction of the blink of an eye. Vandiyadevan had been startled by the simultaneous attack from all sides. He could never have expected it. Now, sitting bound inside the palanquin, he could barely think. There was no way to figure out what the plan was. As they bounced him along though, his mind cleared slowly. The blindfold wasn't hard to dislodge. He manoeuvred his bound hands so he could part the curtain and look outside. They seemed to be taking a shortcut to somewhere, from near the riverbank.

It wouldn't be a hard task to free himself of the ropes that bound his hands and feet. It would then be easy to jump out of the palanquin, grab his horse and make a run for it. He could take on this lot, these seven–eight men who'd only been able to overpower him because of the surprise factor. He wondered if he should go for it. But something stopped him. There was some sort of obstacle.

The interior of the palanquin was perfumed by an ethereal essence. It was, at first, invigorating. He didn't have the heart to leave this scent behind just yet. It was too intoxicating. Where would the palanquin lead him? There was enough indication that it was Nandini who had sent for him. He did have a tiny little craving for just one more meeting with her ... and as time passed, that tiny little craving grew into an all-consuming ache. There were plenty of reasons he shouldn't give in to this desire. And yet, he found ways to rule out each reason, one by one. What could she do to him, anyway? Surely, it couldn't hurt to find out what it was she wanted with him? He might even learn something. He'd got himself out of every scrape in which he'd found himself thus far. Surely, he could counter any trap they set for him, and entrap his opponents instead? He was capable of that much, he knew it. There wasn't much chance he would see her again after this. It was near impossible for him to go to Thanjavur. Simply too dangerous. Much easier to meet her en route. What harm could it possibly do him to meet the Ilaiya Rani, just once more?

Oh ... oh! And there was yet another crucial reason to meet Nandini. The Oomai Rani he had seen in Lanka! Was he right in his assessment that she resembled Nandini closely? He had to verify that, didn't he? He couldn't do that without another close look at the Pazhuvoor Ilaiya Rani's face, now, could he?

Even as these thoughts ran through Vandiyadevan's head, he began to feel lightheaded. Sleep weighed his eyelids down. No, no! This could not be sleep! He had slept almost through the day. No, this was something else, this was … the perfume in the palanquin was some sort of soporific, he thought. No, it was dangerous to stay on here! Aiyo! What peril! He would have to make a run for it!

Vandiyadevan began to undo the ropes that bound his hands. But … no, he couldn't. His fingers wouldn't move. He tried to sit up. He couldn't do that either. He tried to move his legs, but no … his limbs felt like they didn't belong to him anymore. His eyelids were closing. He couldn't think anymore. He was losing consciousness.

~*~

When Vandiyadevan came to, his instinct to jump out of the palanquin was strong. Yes, he could move now! He would jump … but … wonder of wonders! He was no longer in a palanquin. No, he was in an expansive room, brightly lit by the flames of many, many lamps.

This room was perfumed too. But it wasn't the same fragrance he had sensed inside the palanquin. This was heavy smoke, carrying the comforting smell of oil lamps. The old scent had dullened his senses, and this one heightened them. He sat up and took in his surroundings. A door across the room opened just then. Vandiyadevan waited eagerly to see who it was.

Nandini entered through the door. Vandiyadevan couldn't stop staring at her. There were many reasons for his fascination and astonishment. Her beauty, which defied all description, was one. The utter unexpectedness of this encounter was another. Yet another, was the eerie resemblance between the faces and figures of the Oomai Rani from Lanka and this much younger woman. Was it only a resemblance? Or was one of them in disguise?

The Pazhuvoor Ilaiya Rani now smiled and said in a lilting voice, 'Aiya! You're a truly good man.'

'Vandanam!'[1] Vandiyadevan said.

'They say the hallmark of a good man is discretion. And you were so discreet you disappeared from the palace without so much as a goodbye.'

Vandiyadevan laughed.

'I helped you enter the Thanjai palace. I gave you my signet ring. Surely, it would have been good form to return it to me before you left?'

Vandiyadevan was now embarrassed into silence.

'Surely, you can return it at least now, can't you? What use do you have for it? You can't have intentions of coming back to the Thanjavur palace, surely?' Nandini said, and extended an arm opening her palm, smooth and soft as a petal, for the ring.

'Devi! Senapati Boothi Vikrama Kesari confiscated the ring in Lanka. So, I find myself unable to return it to you. Please forgive me,' Vandiyadevan said.

'So, you've handed over the ring I gave you to my mortal enemy. What a show of gratitude!'

'I did not hand it over of my own free will. They forced it from my hands.'

'A scion of the Vaanar clan, the bravest of brave warriors descended from Vaanaathi Rayar, and you gave in to force? Unbelievable!'

'Ammani! I'm here right now by force, aren't I? Your men ...'

'Tell me the truth, aiya! Think back and answer honestly ... was it entirely by force that you were brought here? Was it not from your free will? Did you have no desire to see me? Did you have no opportunity to jump off the palanquin?'

Nandini's questions were as arrows that pierced Vandiyadevan's heart.

'Well, yes. I *am* here of my own free will.'

'To what end?'

'To what end did you have me escorted here?'

'To ask for my ring back.'

'Was that all?'

'There's another reason too. You were in the subterranean passage that night, weren't you? In the rooms that are part of the treasury that falls under my husband's charge?'

Vandiyadevan was startled.

'Did you think I didn't know? Could you have got away that night if it were not for me?'

'Devi ...'

'Oh, yes, I know, I know it all. As does Periya Pazhuvettaraiyar. My husband ordered the guard to have you killed and your corpse disposed of right there. It was I who revoked the order when his back was turned. It is because of me that you got away, and your dear friend got into trouble instead. Otherwise, your bones would have been lying among those precious stones.'

Vandiyadevan was now swimming in a sea of surprise. He couldn't believe that she was telling the truth. But if she wasn't, how could she possibly know the details she did? Well, he supposed custom demanded that he thank her for saving his life. So, he began, 'Ammani ...'

'No, please don't. I don't want you to say anything you don't feel. Please don't try to thank me when you feel no gratitude.'

'No, devi ...'

'Do you know why I let you in on the fact that it was I who saved your life that day? Not from expectation of your gratitude, but to warn you not to use the subterranean passage any longer. It is heavily guarded now.'

'I have no plans of going anywhere near that place.'

'And why should you have such plans? It isn't in your nature to think of those who have helped you, is it? Your friend nearly lost his life because of you. It was I who had him brought to the palace, and I who nursed him back to health before sending him on his way. I hope it makes you happy to hear this. Or, is a penchant for betrayal of friendship inborn in you, along with your propensity for betrayal of trust?'

Nandini's words were as a poisoned potion that stuck in Vandiyadevan's throat and made his heart wilt. His silence came from suffering.

'You ensured the physician's son who accompanied you to Kodikkarai was arrested in your stead. Did you so much as enquire what became of him?'

'I intended to ask you.'

'I'll tell you. But you tell me first, what became of Prince Arulmozhi Varmar who accompanied you from Lanka? I'll tell you about the physician's son if you'll tell me about the prince.'

Vandiyadevan nearly jumped out of his skin. So, it was to learn what had happened to the prince that she had had him brought here. And that was why she had tormented him with her accusations. No, he must not allow her to find a chink in his armour. He would not succumb to her taunts.

'Arasi![2] Please don't ask me about that one thing alone,' he said.

'Oh, of course! I shouldn't ask about that one thing alone! And even if I do, you won't respond. I know that. Well, am I allowed to ask what became of your lover girl? How is she doing? Would you be so kind as to share that with me?'

Vandiyadevan's eyes blazed. 'To whom are you referring? Careful!'

'Aha! I'm careful all right. Please don't think I'm referring to that Pazhaiyarai Maharani. She won't so much as spare you a second glance. You are as dust under her feet. I'm talking about the boatwoman who rowed you to and from Lanka. Isn't Poonguzhali your lover?'

'No, not at all! She introduced me to her lovers, in fact. She showed me the kolli vaai pisaasus that show up at midnight in the marshes of Kodikkarai, and told me those were her lovers.'

'What a lucky girl she is! Her lovers are creatures of light who sparkle before one's eyes. My lovers, on the other hand, are creatures of the dark. They're shapeless and formless. Have you ever spent the darkest hours of the night in a desolate ruin? Have you heard the flapping of wings, and wondered whether the creatures flying about in the dark were bats or owls? My heart is one such desolate ruin, and my lovers are the creatures that fly within. They beat their wings and assault my chest. They brush their feathers against my cheeks. Where do those formless figures come from? And where are they headed? Why do they circle around me over and over again? Aiyo! Do you know?'

Nandini's haunted eyes looked wildly about the room as she spoke.

Vandiyadevan felt his heart melt. He felt unbearably sad. An overwhelming pity for this woman fought for primacy with an overpowering terror that he couldn't quite place.

'Devi! What is this? Calm down!' he said.

'Who do you think you are, to ask me to calm down?' Nandini demanded.

'I'm a poor young man born into the Vaanar clan. And who are you, devi?'

'Who am I? You ask who I am? I don't know who I am, myself. I'm trying to find out. I'm trying to find myself. Are you asking whether I'm human, or a ghost or a ghoul?'

'No, no, I'm asking whether you're a divine being, perhaps an apsara, fallen from the celestial skies because of a curse, or ...'

'Yes! There is a curse upon me. I'm cursed! But I don't know what the curse is. I don't know who I am or what my purpose in life is. Why was I born? All I have is this little hint. Look! Here it is!' and with that, Nandini reached for a sword by her side.

It was newly forged. Its sharp point glinted in the light, and the reflection of the lamps bounced off the blade.

Vandiyadevan stared at the sword. He recognised it right away. This was the sword he had seen at the forgery. Thus far, Nandini's words had hit him like poison. Now, she had brandished a sword. Its iron gave him strength. His heart was fortified by the sight. He understood swords and spears. He had held them for as long as he could remember. He knew them, he had ties with them. He felt no fear of them. Nandini could use the sword against him for all he cared. He would feel no fear.

'Devi! I see it, I see the sword. I see the craftsmanship, and I know it is a royal sword. It is a sword that has been forged to be brandished by intrepid warriors. How did it make its way into your delicate hands? And of what is this a hint to you?' he asked.

# NOTES

## 1. THE 'ELELA SINGHAN' KOOTHU

1   A nutritious dish made of vegetable gravy, rice, and other grains and cereals.

2   A temple erected to commemorate a martyred warrior.

3   Long before the southern region of India was divided into four states, one of which goes by 'Tamil Nadu', Sangam literature referred to a composite of twelve regions, which was known as 'Senthamzhinadu', which translates into 'lush and prosperous Tamil lands'. Although it refers to the same area as Tamizhagam, this word carries a note of pride.

## 2. KILLI VALAVAN'S ELEPHANT

1   Modern-day Polonnaruwa.

2   A reference to the title of 'Kozhi Vendar' with which the Chozha kings styled themselves.

## 4. ANURADHAPURAM

1   Temple festival.

2   Also known as Janmashtami and Krishna Jayanti, this festival celebrates the birth of the god Krishna.

3   While this word has many connotations now, it originally implied the surrender of one kingdom to another. It symbolised a transfer of power, and the sengol was an ornate gold sceptre that bound its holder to rule with righteousness and impartiality.

4   One of the five *Perungaappiyams* or great epics of ancient Tamil literature, this book—believed to have been written by a young Jain prince who only goes by Ilangovadigal, which means 'younger prince', suggesting he had an older brother who was heir to the throne—tells the story of a merchant Kovalan, his involvement with the courtesan Madhavi and his fiery wife Kannagi. Kovalan is wrongfully accused of stealing the queen's anklet and put to death for the sin. A tad excessive, one must admit. Kannagi storms into the court and matches the king's bloodlust with her own pyromania. Having proven her husband's innocence, of theft if not infidelity, she goes on to burn down Madurai. For some reason, this woman who set thousands of strangers on fire for a pronouncement made by one man—and all this for a philandering husband—is worshipped as a goddess in Tamil Nadu.

5   The accepted spelling of the king's name is 'Duttugemunu' or 'Dutugamunu'. In Tamil, it is usually spelt 'Duttakaamini'. However, Kalki uses the spelling 'Dushtakamanu' and so I have gone with this variation.

## 5. THE LANKAN THRONE

1   A polite form of address for a devotee, particularly one who has devoted his life to the service, of a god.

## 6. 'WHO VALUES ONE'S WORTH?'

1    This refers to a legend about the Pallava king, Nandi Varman III. The king was a storied ruler, and his three elder stepbrothers were jealous of him. Their wiles included employing manta-tantra as well as warfare, but they could not defeat him. His youngest stepbrother, a poet, was a Tamil scholar and decided to go with the tradition of 'arampaadudal'—to curse someone through language. To that effect, he composed the *Nandi Kalambagam*. The tradition of arampaadudal is quite chilling. It has to do with the hidden meanings of words. A word that appears beautiful and positive might carry a sinister meaning. It is the trickery of words that undoes the listener.

For instance, the opening line of the *Nandi Kalambagam* contains the word 'mandalam', which carries the apparent meaning of 'world'. However, if one were to split the word into 'mandu kootta alam', it would mean 'bereft of mangalam and therefore, inauspicious'. Similarly, the first song contains the phrase 'Ulagudaiyaan tirumudiyum'. If one were to split the second word as 'tirumudi' and 'um', it would refer to 'the hallowed hair of he who has conquered the world'. But if one were to split it as 'tiru' and 'mudiyum', it would mean 'his wealth will be destroyed' or 'his reign will end'. The fifty-third stanza contains the phrase 'kariyaan enra manna'. Here, 'kari' could be interpreted as 'exemplary', and then the phrase would mean 'the king who sets an example for the entire world'. But one could also interpret it as 'ashes', and then the phrase would mean 'the king who burns to death'.

The story goes that, having composed this set of poems, the stepbrother lost all interest in governance and decided to become an ascetic. He would go door to door, asking for alms and singing songs. Sometimes, he sang verses from the *Nandi Kalambagam* too. Eventually, he reached Kanchipuram, the capital of Nandi Varman's kingdom. A woman who heard these verses imbibed them so deeply that she began to sing them herself.

Once when the king's soldiers were on their rounds, they happened to hear her. They told the king about these verses, and he asked that the woman be brought to him. The woman told him the source of the song, prompting the king to launch a search for the ascetic.

The king's men eventually located the ascetic and brought him to court. The king asked the man who he was. Upon learning the ascetic was his own stepbrother, the king was overjoyed. He asked to hear the entire *Nandi Kalambagam*. However, the ascetic refused. When the king insisted, the ascetic explained why.

There was a protocol in place for a king who wished to hear such songs, he said. First, a hundred tents made of palmyra leaves would have to be erected. The king would have to sit under each one in turn and hear a single verse. Once the verse was sung, the tent would spontaneously catch fire, and the king would have to move to the next. For the final verse, the poles that had held up the previous tents and the ashes from the leaves would have to be collected to build a pyre of sorts. The king must sit on these cinders to hear the last verse. Once the verse had been sung, the pyre would catch fire and the king would burn on the pile of cinders. The ascetic begged to be excused from singing this final verse at least.

However, the king was so in love with Tamil poetry that he insisted on hearing them all, even at the cost of his life. The heartbreaking final verse goes:

*Vaanoru madhiyai adaindhadhu un vadanam*
*Maraikadal pugundhadhu un keerthi*
*Kaanoru puliyai adaindhadhu on veeram*
*Karpagam adaindhadhu un karangal*
*Thenuru malaraal ariyidam pugundaal*
*Senthazhal adaindhadhu un deham*
*Naanum en kaliyum evvidum puguvom*
*Nandiye nandayaabarane!*

*Your lovely countenance now illuminates the sky*
*Your glory has sunk into the depth of the oceans*
*Your courage has graced the tiger in the forest*
*Your hands have been touched by divine camphor*
*She who sits in the flower that brews honey (Lakshmi)*
*Has become one with Hari (Vishnu), knowing the world*
  *has ended*
*Your body has been consigned to fire on these burning*
  *cinders*
*Where will my poverty and I go,*
*O Nandi, you jewel of your clan!*

Nandi Varman III is often referred to as 'the king who sacrificed his life for Tamil', because his love for the language superseded his will to live.

## 7. KAVERI AMMAN

1   Modern-day Elephant Pass, the site of several battles over the centuries—most recently three devastating ones of the Sri Lankan Civil War in the 1990s and 2000s—located as it is in a strategic spot, the gateway of the Jaffna peninsula.

## 9. 'HERE'S YOUR WAR!'

1   The three speeds in a musical composition, going from one strike per beat to four strikes per beat.
2   Several of the Pandiya kings had the name 'Veerapandiyan'. The king whom Boothi Vikrama Kesari beheaded is likely a forebear of the Pandiya king whom Aditya Karikalan beheaded.
3   Parthibendran was part of Aditya Karikalan's party when they had hunted down Veerapandiyan, and this seems to entitle him to sharing the credit for the beheading.
4   'Kunjaram' means 'elephant' and 'mallan' is 'wrestler'. The composite word 'Kunjaramallan' could be interpreted either as a warrior capable of defeating elephants barehanded, or as a wrestler as powerful as an elephant.

## 10. A CONFERENCE

1   This is drawn from a hilarious Tamil idiom, 'Rudraksha poonai upadesam panninathu polai', which translates

literally into 'Like a cat wearing rudraksha beads and preaching scripture.' The folktale behind this has variations across India. The best-known version is that a cat once pretended to be involved in great penance by the river Ganga. He put on such an act of piety that the birds and mice began to worship him. One day, he opened his eyes and declared that he was too weak to walk to the river to bathe, and that his followers must carry him. He allowed this bed of prey to escort him to the river and then pounced on them. A suspicious mouse called Killika, who'd had the foresight to spy on him, ran back to warn the other potential prey, who then fled, forcing the cat to move his act elsewhere. The idiom is often used to speak of 'godmen' who use religion for their own ends.

## 11. 'LOOK, OVER THERE!'

1   In one of many examples of discontinuity in the text, the original reads, 'The man reached casually for his dagger even as he was speaking, and flung it at a bush.' Later, we come to learn that he reached for Poonguzhali's dagger. This, to me, is evidence of Kalki writing almost faster than he could think, with no time to refer to what he had written earlier, because the immense popularity of the series demanded that he write a chapter a week in order for the magazine to continue to sell at the rate it was.

## 12. POONGUZHALI'S DAGGER

1   'Paavi' literally means 'sinner'. The closest translation of 'Paavi penne' would be 'wretched woman', but it

is used lightly here, which is why I chose to retain the original.

## 14. 'THE ELEPHANT HAS GONE ROGUE!'

1    This is a reference to an episode in the Ramayana, where Hanuman is tasked with crossing the seas and a few thousand miles to fetch the Sanjeevni herb to save Lakshman's life. Unable to identify the herb on the mountain on which it grew, Hanuman lifted the entire mountain and carried it to Lakshman's side.

## 15. THE PRISON SHIP

1    The lord of the devas, Indra.

2    A grinding wheel, typically used to cold press oils.

3    This word translates literally into 'elder mother', and—along with 'Periyamma'—could refer to several people: one's mother's older sister; one's father's older brother's wife; and in case one is the offspring of a second wife, one's father's first wife.

4    The story of Valli's marriage to Muruga in the Kanda Puranam—the Tamil iteration of the Skanda Purana— has him taking on various guises in an attempt to woo her. Valli, who has been told that she is destined to be the wife of Lord Muruga, is enraged by every other suitor and turns each down cruelly. Muruga then takes the form of an old man and hangs about while Ganesha takes the form of a wild elephant and charges at Valli. For some reason, the agile Valli—who, in the current avatar, is the daughter of a tribal chieftain and a skilled huntress—turns to the old man for help. The old man agrees to help her on the condition of marriage, to

which Valli acquiesces out of fear for her life. The story ends happily when the old man turns out to be Muruga, who—unlike several other gods—is not offended by the fact that her will to live trumped her love for him.

## 16.  BRIMMING WITH JOY

1   Father's sister. In some contexts, it is used to mean 'mother-in-law', but not in this case.

2   A gesture of respect towards one's elders, but this is a remarkable act for a prince, since his social status would preclude a show of such obeisance except to elders in his own family or his gurus. This might be why the woman is so touched by the act.

3   This is a reference to an incident from the Mahabharata, during Arjuna's time as Brihannala. He acts as the tutor of Uttara, who would eventually become his daughter-in-law. Her brother Uttara Kumar had never known war, since his father had ensured he was cossetted in the palace at all times. When he eventually had to fight off a Kaurava attack, he was terrified. Brihannala was his charioteer, and did the fighting on his behalf. It all ended happily, but Uttara Kumar's show of cowardice is often used as a lesson in poor upbringing.

4   The unspoken ending to this line is '… like a woman'. While this might appear regressive in today's era where we speak of gender equality, we must admit the Chozha empire might not have become the powerful empire it became, if the princes had been kept away from the battlefield and confined to their palaces and their pleasures.

5    'Kili' means 'parrot' and 'thozhi' means 'female friend'. In ancient Tamil poetry and folklore, the heroine's friend often carried messages from the heroine to her lover. A talking parrot would, naturally, be a useful friend and ally, armed with the twin powers of speech and flight. However, the heroines of Tamil poetry tended to use the parrot more as a therapist—or more accurately, soundboard—than a messenger, choosing instead to send their two-legged, unwinged friends on thankless journeys to the hero.

## 19. HUNT FOR THE SHIP

1    Refers to the sin of betrayal of friendship.

## 20. THE ABATHTHUDAVIGAL

1    Like the Velakkara Army of the Chozha kings, the Pandiyas have this elite force in their ranks. However, since Kalki says they are not trained warriors, one must assume they are spies, or perhaps a squad comprising people with various skills that might be needed in this elite band.

2    The wind instrument used by snake charmers to make snakes 'dance'.

## 21. WHIRLWINDS

1    'Anna' is older brother, and 'thambi' is younger brother. The latter is often used to address a stranger who happens to be younger. Vandiyadevan is mocking Ravidasan here, by addressing him as 'anna' in response to the 'thambi'.

2　In the original Tamil version, Kalki used the term 'Kumbakonam', which is a more modern spelling, in some places. However, in the interest of avoiding confusion for readers, I have used 'Kudandai' throughout.

3　The Tamil word used here is 'andagadaagam', which is an imaginary shell surrounding the universe as the ancients understood it, some sort of compendium of several lower and higher worlds (usually agreed upon as fourteen in all).

4　I chose to retain the original word rather than go with, say 'flood' or 'deluge', because of the mythological connotations that capture its epic scale.

5　The five elements are often referred to as 'pancha bhoota' in literature—Prithvi (Earth), Agni (Fire), Varuna or Apa (Water), Vayu (Wind) and Aakasha (Space/Aether).

## 23. SONG OF SOLACE

1　The 'sangu' is the conch and 'chakra' the discus of the Hindu god Vishnu. With astrologers and laypeople claiming they could see these emblems on the prince's hands, it was believed he was under special divine protection.

2　'Samhara' refers to killing, usually in a violent form. One of the visions of Doomsday in Tamil literature is of a vengeant god out to destroy all humanity, while demons dance around him. This god is presumably called 'Samhara Murti'. Or, since 'murti' means 'statue', it could be that the demons are worshipping

a statue of this god even as he goes about his business—
destruction.

3    Friend

## AN EXTRACT FROM BOOK 5: DEATHLY SWORD

1    This is an elaborate greeting, hilariously ironic in the
current context. One rarely uses it except in the
presence of a king or guru. The movements that a
dance or traditional martial arts exponent performs as
obeisance to the gods before beginning a performance
tend to be called 'vandanam'.

2    'Arasi' and 'Rani' are used interchangeably.